◁ Y0-BCT-994

Uninvited Guests

As the door slammed open, Clint reacted instantly from reflex. He lifted the girl off him and dropped her on the other side of the bed, so she'd be protected. Then he grabbed his gun from the holster on the bedpost. By the time the two men burst into the room, he had his gun trained on the door.

As Joe and Johnny Crespo rushed into the room, they saw that their idea had not been such a good one, after all. But they had their guns in their hands, and there was only one way to react. They pulled their triggers.

The brothers' shots, fired in haste, sprayed the room. Clint calmly fired back, striking each brother in the chest, precisely in the heart. They both fell to the floor, dead.

The girl—Amy or Delores, whichever name she wanted to use—stuck her head up from behind the bed and said, "Is it over?"

Bruce County Public Library
1243 Mackenzie Rd.
Port Elgin ON N0H 2C6

DON'T MISS THESE
ALL-ACTION WESTERN SERIES
FROM THE BERKLEY PUBLISHING GROUP

THE GUNSMITH by J. R. Roberts

Clint Adams was a legend among lawmen, outlaws, and ladies. They called him . . . the Gunsmith.

LONGARM by Tabor Evans

The popular long-running series about Deputy U.S. Marshal Custis Long—his life, his loves, his fight for justice.

SLOCUM by Jake Logan

Today's longest-running action Western. John Slocum rides a deadly trail of hot blood and cold steel.

BUSHWHACKERS by B. J. Lanagan

An action-packed series by the creators of Longarm! The rousing adventures of the most brutal gang of cutthroats ever assembled—Quantrill's Raiders.

DIAMONDBACK by Guy Brewer

Dex Yancey is Diamondback, a Southern gentleman turned con man when his brother cheats him out of the family fortune. Ladies love him. Gamblers hate him. But nobody pulls one over on Dex . . .

WILDGUN by Jack Hanson

The blazing adventures of mountain man Will Barlow— from the creators of Longarm!

TEXAS TRACKER by Tom Calhoun

J.T. Law: the most relentless—and dangerous—manhunter in all Texas. Where sheriffs and posses fail, he's the best man to bring in the most vicious outlaws—for a price.

THE GUNSMITH

361

THE LETTER OF THE LAW

J. R. ROBERTS

JOVE BOOKS, NEW YORK

THE BERKLEY PUBLISHING GROUP
Published by the Penguin Group
Penguin Group (USA) Inc.
375 Hudson Street, New York, New York 10014, USA
Penguin Group (Canada), 90 Eglinton Avenue East, Suite 700, Toronto, Ontario M4P 2Y3, Canada
(a division of Pearson Penguin Canada Inc.)
Penguin Books Ltd., 80 Strand, London WC2R 0RL, England
Penguin Group Ireland, 25 St. Stephen's Green, Dublin 2, Ireland (a division of Penguin Books Ltd.)
Penguin Group (Australia), 250 Camberwell Road, Camberwell, Victoria 3124, Australia
(a division of Pearson Australia Group Pty. Ltd.)
Penguin Books India Pvt. Ltd., 11 Community Centre, Panchsheel Park, New Delhi—110 017, India
Penguin Group (NZ), 67 Apollo Drive, Rosedale, Auckland 0632, New Zealand
(a division of Pearson New Zealand Ltd.)
Penguin Books (South Africa) (Pty.) Ltd., 24 Sturdee Avenue, Rosebank, Johannesburg 2196,
South Africa

Penguin Books Ltd., Registered Offices: 80 Strand, London WC2R 0RL, England

This is a work of fiction. Names, characters, places, and incidents either are the product of the author's imagination or are used fictitiously, and any resemblance to actual persons, living or dead, business establishments, events, or locales is entirely coincidental

THE LETTER OF THE LAW

A Jove Book / published by arrangement with the author

PRINTING HISTORY
Jove edition / January 2012

Copyright © 2012 by Robert J. Randisi.
Cover illustration by Sergio Giovine.

All rights reserved.
No part of this book may be reproduced, scanned, or distributed in any printed or electronic form without permission. Please do not participate in or encourage piracy of copyrighted materials in violation of the author's rights. Purchase only authorized editions.
For information, address: The Berkley Publishing Group,
a division of Penguin Group (USA) Inc.,
375 Hudson Street, New York, New York 10014.

ISBN: 978-0-515-15030-8

JOVE®
Jove Books are published by The Berkley Publishing Group,
a division of Penguin Group (USA) Inc.,
375 Hudson Street, New York, New York 10014.
JOVE® is a registered trademark of Penguin Group (USA) Inc.
The "J" design is a trademark of Penguin Group (USA) Inc.

PRINTED IN THE UNITED STATES OF AMERICA

10 9 8 7 6 5 4 3 2 1

If you purchased this book without a cover, you should be aware that this book is stolen property. It was reported as "unsold and destroyed" to the publisher, and neither the author nor the publisher has received any payment for this "stripped book."

ONE

As Clint rode into the town of Adobe Walls, in Hutchison County, Texas, his mind went back to the original settlement some miles away, the site of the Second Battle of Adobe Walls, where he and a band of 28 settlers held off 700 Indians for 3 days until Billy Dixon—longtime buffalo hunter and scout—completely demoralized the enemy by borrowing a Sharps Big .50 and shooting an Indian cleanly off his horse from a distance of almost a mile away. It became known as "The Shot of the Century."

Since then, Billy Dixon had gone on to become an Army scout and eventually win the Congressional Medal of Honor for another famous battle known as the Buffalo Wallow Fight.

Clint had heard that Dixon, retired from the Army and—apparently—from carrying a gun, had taken a job in the town of Adobe Walls. Since he was nearby, he decided to stop in and see his friend and catch up.

Fully intending to stop in town for a few days, Clint rode

directly to the livery stable and turned his horse, Eclipse, over to the liveryman, who—as always—was suitably impressed.

The few minutes in a new town were always spent the same way. Clint sometimes wished there was a way to skip all that—the livery, then carrying saddle and rifle to a nearby hotel to register and get a room. Most of the time the rooms were little more than satisfactory, unless he had been sleeping on the trail for an extended period of time. In that case, almost any bed was an improvement over the hard ground. And while he enjoyed trail food, he usually rode into town—any town—in search of a good steak.

He went through all the motions, and then stopped into the first saloon he saw for a good beer and some advice . . .

"What can I getcha?" the barkeep asked.

"A cold beer."

"Comin' up."

The bartender, a young man with a spring in his step, set a brimming mug down in front of Clint without spilling a drop.

"New in town, huh?"

"That's right."

"My name's Chris. Can I help you with anythin' else? A woman maybe?"

"Nope."

"Well, I can pretty much get you anythin' you want in this town—"

"I'm just interested in seeing your postmaster."

"The postmaster? We got one of them?"

"I believe you do," Clint said.

The man frowned and scratched his head.

"What's a postmaster do?"

"He runs the post office," Clint said. When Chris still looked confused, he added, "He takes care of the mail."

"Oh, the mail!" Chris said. "Is that what he's called? Postmaster?"

"That's right."

"Well, I'll be damned."

"So about the only thing you can help me with is finding the post office."

The bartender looked confused again.

"That's okay," Clint said. "I'll find it myself."

"Well, if there's anything else you want," Chris said, "you just let me know."

"I sure will," Clint said, "seeing as how you've been so helpful this time."

TWO

Clint left the saloon after one beer and went in search of the post office. He could have asked the hotel clerk, but he didn't think of it at the time. In the end he simply stopped a likely-looking woman—someone who looked like she sent and received mail—and asked where the post office was.

"It's three streets that way," she said, pointing.

"Thank you."

"Would you be lookin' for some company later?"

He stared at her. He'd stopped her because she looked respectable. Now he looked harder. She was blond, in her thirties, with a knowing glint in her eye. A prostitute, and making an offer to him right on the street.

"Um, I don't think so."

"Well," she said, "if you're in town long enough and you decide you do, come and find me at Miss Lily's. My name's Peggy."

"Peggy," he said. "I'll remember. Thanks for the directions."

"Any time."

She flounced off and he followed her directions to a small storefront that housed the U.S. Post Office. Next to the door was a wooden shingle that said, WILLIAM DIXON, POSTMASTER.

He went inside.

A mustached man was standing behind a wooden counter, sorting through mail and sliding it into the appropriate slots behind him. He was in shirtsleeves, held up by garters, and wearing a visor.

Clint waited a few minutes for him to turn around, but when he didn't, he said, "Hey, Billy."

"With you in a minute," Dixon said over his shoulder—then he seemed to notice that someone had called him "Billy" and not "William." He turned his head and looked over his shoulder this time.

"Clint?"

Clint smiled.

"Clint Adams?"

He put down the mail in his hands and turned around to face Clint.

"By God, it is you!" he exclaimed. He came out from behind the counter and rushed forward, grabbed Clint's hand, and began pumping it.

"How you doing, Billy?"

"Great, great," Dixon said. "How the hell are you?"

"Good."

"It's been a while."

"Yeah, it has," Clint said. "Never expected to find you working at the post office, though."

"I'm not working at the post office," Dixon said. "I'm running the post office."

Clint looked Dixon up and down. Late thirties now, looked to be in good shape. No apparent injuries. And no gun.

"Running the post office?" Clint repeated. "But . . . why?"

"I got tired of making my way with a gun," Dixon said. "I've got a ranch near here—actually, right on the site of Adobe Walls—and I'd been living here awhile when they offered me this job."

"Who offered it to you?"

"The government."

"So, how long . . ."

"I've only been postmaster for a few months. What are you doing here?"

"I was near here, so I rode out to your ranch to see you. Your foreman told me you were here, working as the postmaster. So I came to see for myself."

Dixon stepped back and spread his arms.

"So what do you think?"

"I'm not used to seeing you without a gun," Clint said. "And . . ."

"And what?"

"Well . . . you're so clean."

"That's because I don't spend that much time on the trail anymore. You, though . . ."

"What?"

"You could use a bath and a change of clothes. Just get here?"

Clint nodded. "Just had time to take care of my horse

and get a room. Why don't we go get something to eat?"

"I'm the postmaster," Dixon said. "And I work here alone. I can't just leave . . . but we can meet at five and then get something to eat."

"That's three hours."

"Well, if you're hungry, go and have something small," Dixon said. "Meet me back here and I'll take you for the best steak in town. Whataya say?"

"That sounds like a good deal," Clint said. "Can you tell me where I can get a good slice of peach pie?"

THREE

Dixon had not steered Clint wrong.

He'd given him directions to a small café a couple of blocks away, where he got a piece of the best peach pie he'd had in a while. If only the coffee had been as good. It needed to be stronger, but it was okay to wash down the pie.

"Anythin' else?" the waiter asked.

"Nope," Clint said. "That was what I needed."

He paid the waiter, who told him to come back when he was hungry again.

"I'll do that," Clint said. "Thanks."

Clint left the café, still having better than two hours to kill before meeting with Dixon. He decided he might as well spend some of it finding out who the law in Adobe Walls was.

He found the sheriff's office and went inside. It was typical of sheriffs' and marshals' offices in smaller towns in the

West. Larger Western cities were setting up more modern police departments, but Adobe Walls still depended on a sheriff to keep the peace.

He heard the sound of a broom then saw a man come out of the cell block, wielding the broom and wearing the badge.

"Sheriff?"

The man's head whipped up, and he looked surprised.

"Didn't hear you come in," he grunted.

"Sorry if I startled you."

The man straightened up, leaned on the broom. He was a thick-bodied man in his forties. The star on his chest was showing wear—dents, and a bit pitted.

"Sheriff Garver. What can I do for you?" the sheriff asked.

"My name's Clint Adams, just got into town a while ago," Clint said. "I got a room in the Stetson Hotel."

"Adams?"

"That's right."

The sheriff chewed his mustache for a moment.

"The Gunsmith?"

"Right again."

"What brings you to town, Mr. Adams?"

"Friend of mine works here," Clint said. "I came to visit him."

"And who would that friend be?"

"Billy Dixon," Clint said, then added, "your postmaster."

"Dixon, huh?" the sheriff said.

"The hero of Adobe Walls."

"If you say so." The man didn't say so with any kind of feeling.

"I don't say so," Clint said. "I was there."

"That so?"

"That so."

The sheriff shrugged. "Well, then, you oughtta know, right?"

"Right."

He started working the broom again.

"You ain't come to town to cause trouble, have ya?" the sheriff asked.

"I never come to town to cause trouble."

"But it follows you."

Clint shrugged. "If you say so," he commented. "All I know is I came here to see Dixon."

"Gonna stay long?"

"A few days maybe."

"Well," the lawman said, leaning on the broom again, "have a good time."

"Thanks, I will."

Clint walked to the door and went out without further word.

The lawman leaned on the broom until Clint was gone. When the door closed, he leaned the broom against the wall and went into the cell block. Only one cell was occupied. He unlocked the door and woke the occupant up.

"Come on, Lenny." He shook the man.

"Hey—wha—that you, Sheriff?"

Lenny Wilson stared owlishly up at Garver.

"It's me, Lenny. Come up, stand up."

Wilson had been in the cell since the night before and still smelled like whiskey. He was relatively sober, though.

Garver got him to his feet and walked him into the office. He poured him a cup of coffee and sat him down with it.

"Drink it," he said. "I want you to understand what I'm sayin'."

"Okay, okay," Wilson said. "I'm listenin'."

"I want you to leave here and go find Al Wycliffe. You got that?"

"Yeah, I got it," Wilson said. "Al."

Wilson was about six-two and weighed about one-forty when he had a heavy beard stubble, which he had now.

"You know where to find him, right?"

"He could be in two or three places."

"Well, you check them all, huh?"

"Sure, sure . . ." Wilson put the coffee down.

"How about a drink, Sheriff?"

Garver stared at Wilson, then opened his desk drawer. He took out a bottle of whiskey. Wilson reached for it, but Garver simply poured some into the man's coffee and then put the bottle away.

"Aw, Sheriff—"

"That's all you get, and don't stop for any more until you deliver my message. You sabe?"

"I got you." He picked up the cup and drank the combination down greedily.

"Now go!" Garver barked. "Tell Al we got to call it off, and he should come and see me. Got it?"

"Got it. Call it off and come see you."

"Go ahead."

"How about a little—" Wilson said, extending the cup.

Garver grabbed it from his hand and said, "Go!"

He watched as Wilson went out the door. As it slammed, he was thinking, this was the wrong time for the Gunsmith to show up.

FOUR

Clint met Dixon in front of the post office as the man locked the door.

"Anything of value in there?" he asked.

"Letters, my friend," Dixon said. "Just letters."

They started walking.

"You know, I really liked it when the pony express was operating," Clint said.

"They figured out a better way real quick," Dixon reminded him. "You can't believe how fast the mail gets cross-country now."

"Yeah, well, I don't get much mail," Clint said.

"You don't stay in one place long enough for a letter to reach you."

"That's true."

"Turn here," Dixon said. "This place has the best steaks in town."

"Yeah," Clint said, "but does that mean that they're good?"

"You'll find out."

*   *   *

The steaks were good. Once again, however, as with the café, the coffee was lacking.

"Is there good coffee in town?" Clint asked.

"What's wrong with this coffee?" Dixon asked.

"Not strong enough."

"That's right. You like that really strong trail goop that you make."

"I make good coffee."

"Yeah," Dixon said, "if you want to get the paint off a building."

"Shut up and eat your steak."

Over the meal they caught up with each other. Dixon, while younger than Clint, had become weary of the life of a scout, a life in the saddle, which was why he'd decided to become a rancher, and then a postmaster.

"Did you say you were at the hotel?" Dixon asked.

"Yes, the Stetson."

"Why don't you come back to the ranch with me and stay there? It'll save you some money."

"Have you got a wife?"

"What? A wife? No, no wife. Just me and some ranch hands."

"In the morning you'll have to come back here to the post office, right?"

"Right."

"Well, no offense, but I think I'd rather be in town so I can find something to do."

"Yeah," Dixon said, "I can see where you'd want that. You gonna stay long?"

"I've ridden a long way, so I thought I'd let my horse rest a few days."

"Good," Dixon said. "We still have time to catch up."

"Right."

"Maybe play some poker."

"You got a game going?"

"Nothing regular, but I'm sure there are games in the saloons."

"How many saloons?"

"Three that have gaming," Dixon said, "a couple just for drinkin'. A whorehouse, too, but you still don't use those, do you?"

"No."

"Never understood that myself, but then you've never had a shortage of women, have you?"

"I guess not," Clint said.

"How's that work?"

Clint shrugged. "Women like me."

"That's obvious," Dixon said. "They don't like me much."

"Why do you think that is?"

"I don't know how to talk to them," Dixon said. "Even when a woman comes into the post office, I get nervous. So whores are good enough for me. You don't have to talk to them."

"I suppose that'd be a plus in your situation," Clint said.

"How is it you know what to say to 'em?" Dixon asked.

Clint shrugged and answered, "I just say what comes into my head."

"And it's the right thing?"

"Usually."

"You're lucky, then."

Clint decided to change the subject from women.

"I dropped in on your sheriff."

"Garver?" Dixon said with a look of distaste. "He's not much of a lawman. In fact, I think he's downright crooked."

"Can you prove it?"

"I don't want to," Dixon said. "It's not my job."

"You can live in a town where you know the law is crooked?"

"Long as I don't have to deal with him," Dixon said. "Look, I stay at my ranch, or I stay in the post office. I don't go lookin' for trouble."

"I suppose I can understand that," Clint said. "You've had your share over the years."

"And most of the time I went lookin' for it," Dixon said. "Like scoutin' for the Army. That's just always lookin' for trouble."

"And hunting buffalo?"

"Now that was the life," Dixon said. "As long as you weren't greedy and left enough for the Indians, but men like you, me, and Bat Masterson were the only ones who wasn't greedy. And now the buffalo are gone."

"I know," Clint said, shaking his head, "it's a damn shame."

Dixon nodded his agreement, and they ordered pie.

FIVE

They left the café, and Dixon took Clint to one of the saloons that didn't have gaming. They wanted a quiet place to have a beer and continue talking.

The saloon was called the Big Tap Saloon, and when they entered, Clint saw why. It was fairly small, but the bar filled almost half the room, and the beer taps themselves were huge. Clint only hoped the beer itself matched the bar and the taps—and it did. It was cold, and smooth.

"Best beer in town," Dixon said. "If you want games and girls, though, you go to one of the bigger places."

"I stopped into one of those earlier, without even noticing the name," Clint said. "The bartender was a young guy who thought I needed a girl."

"You were probably in the Tumbleweed," Dixon said. "The bartenders there are pretty aggressive."

"The Tumbleweed?"

"Yeah, I know," Dixon said, "not very original."

"This beer is good," Clint said. He paused to look around

the place. It looked like there were only eight to ten tables, but they all had two or three people at them.

"Yeah, most of the men around here want the action of the girls and the games, so you can usually get a table or bar space here."

"So," Clint asked, "how long do you think you'll be doing this postmaster job?"

Lenny Wilson finally found Al Wycliffe holed up in a room with a whore. It wasn't a hotel or a whorehouse, but the girl's own room. Somebody told him they saw Wycliffe with the girl and where she lived.

The girl was a tall, skinny whore named Patty. She worked in the whorehouse, but she had special "clients" that she took home with her, and Wycliffe was one of them.

Wycliffe liked Patty because she was tall and had amazingly long legs. He especially liked to hold her by the ankles, spread her, and fuck her like that. Those legs seemed to reach all the way to the ceiling, and it excited him to spread-eagle her like that.

Wycliffe was a big man, and while Patty didn't mind it when he did that to her, sometimes she thought he'd get carried away and break her in two. It actually wouldn't have been a bad way to go, though, because when he held her that way, his big dick seemed to hit her in just the right spot when he drove it into her. And he was the only man who fucked her in this fashion.

They were both thoroughly engrossed in what they were doing when the knock came on the door.

Wycliffe grabbed his gun from a nearby table, turned,

and fired a shot through the door, then put the gun down and grabbed Patty's ankles again.

Outside the door as he knocked, Lenny Wilson—nobody's fool—stepped to the side just as a bullet punched through the door.

"Jesus, Al!" he shouted.

"Go away!" Wycliffe yelled back from inside.

"But I got a message for you from the sheriff!" Lenny called back.

No answer.

"If I don't deliver it, he's gonna give me hell!"

Lenny heard voices from inside, low at first, and then raised . . .

"Jesus, Al," Patty said, glaring up at her lover, "can't you get him to go away? I'm tryin' to concentrate here!"

"I'm tryin'," he said.

"Well," she said, "whatever you do about him, don't you dare stop doin' what you're doin' to me!"

"Damn it! he thought.

"What the hell is it, Lenny?" he called, still fucking Patty. "Just yell it out."

From outside the door Lenny yelled, "The sheriff says you should hold off on your plans, and come and see him as soon as you can."

"Okay," Wycliffe said. "You delivered the message. Now get outta here!"

"Oh, baby, yeah," Patty said, "come on, harder, do it harder . . ."

"I'll do it harder all right, bitch," he growled back at her.

Wycliffe knew that Patty used whore talk on her clients, but when she spoke to him during sex, he knew she meant what she said.

He gripped her ankles tighter and started to ram his hard cock into her sopping pussy faster, and faster, and harder . . .

Lenny listened at the door for a few moments, heard the sound of two people grunting. Then he moved to the door and pressed his eye to the hole Al Wycliffe had shot in it.

He could see Wycliffe from the back, covered with coarse hair, holding an ankle in each hand, butt cheeks clenching and unclenching as he drove himself into the girl.

Lenny watched for a while, massaging his own crotch, and when he had an erection, he turned away from the door and hurried out of the building.

As soon as he told the sheriff he'd delivered his message, he was going to head over to Miss Lily's whorehouse. She had one girl he could afford when he really needed one. She wasn't that pretty, she had a harelip, and she was flat as a board, but she had a wet pussy, and at the moment, that was all he cared about.

SIX

Lenny Wilson rushed into the sheriff's office and said, "I found 'im, and gave him yer message."

He turned and started to go back out the door, but Garver yelled, "Whoa, hey, hold it."

Lenny stopped.

"Did he say he was comin'?"

"Um, he didn't say . . . when."

"What was he doin' when you found him?"

"Fuckin' that skinny whore, Patty."

"Great," Garver sad. "He could be doin' that all night."

"I delivered yer message," Lenny said anxiously. "Can I go?"

"Yeah, yeah," Garver said, waving the man away, "you can go. Go on, get outta here!"

Lenny rushed out the door, slamming it behind him.

Probably heading for the nearest saloon, Garver speculated. Come to think of it, he could use a drink himself.

* * *

Sheriff Garver drank in only one saloon in town. It was the other saloon that had no games, so while Clint and Dixon were at the Big Tap, Garver was down the street in Little Jim's Saloon.

Little Jim himself tended bar. There was nothing misleading about his name. He was about five-three, weighed about one-forty. He ruled his place with an iron hand and nobody ever crossed him—except the occasional stranger. Garver had once seen him single-handedly clean three guys out of his place with his bare hands—they were six-footers, and had guns. It didn't matter.

"Sheriff," Jim said as Garver stopped at the bar. "Beer or whiskey?"

"Beer tonight, Jim."

"Comin' up."

At the moment there were only three other men in the saloon. Jim didn't care. He didn't use the saloon to make money. He used it to have something to do. His mother always told him that idle hands were the devil's workshop, and she was right. If he didn't have something to do, he always ended up killing somebody.

"Heard the Gunsmith was in town," Jim said, setting the beer down in front of the lawman.

"That's right," Garver said. "How did you know?"

Jim just gave the sheriff a blank look. He knew everything that went on in town.

"Also heard you was lookin' for Wycliffe."

"That's right."

"Well, he's probably pokin' Patty about now. Usually comes in here when he's done."

Garver nodded.

"Adams stayin' long?" Jim asked.

"Don't know," Garver said. "He's got a friend in town."

"Yeah," Jim said around a toothpick, "Billy Dixon."

Garver shook his head.

"You know everythin'," he said.

"That's right," Jim said. "I know Adams bein' in town changes things."

"Yeah, it does."

"Then maybe somebody should kill him."

"You volunteerin'?"

"Sheriff," Jim said, "you know I never volunteer for nothin'."

"I know that."

"But that don't mean I wouldn't do it."

SEVEN

"What did you tell Garver?" Dixon asked.

Clint looked up from his beer.

"Nothing," he said. "Well, I told him I was here to see you, and that I'd probably be here a few days."

"And?"

"And that I wasn't looking for trouble."

"Are you ever?" Dixon asked. "That don't mean it don't find you. Word's gonna get around, you know. In fact, it probably already has."

"I can't do anything about that," Clint said. "I don't look for trouble, Billy, but that doesn't mean I'm not ready when it comes."

"I know that," Dixon said.

"You worried about the sheriff trying something?" Clint asked.

"I don't know," Dixon said with a shrug. "I don't know him that well."

"You know him well enough to call him dirty."

"That's just from things I've heard," Dixon said. "You know who people talk to the most in town?"

"Bartenders."

"And after that? The postmaster."

"Ah."

"They complain about their husbands, their wives, their kids, the mayor, and the sheriff."

"What's wrong with the mayor?"

"He's crooked, too."

"That figures. Don't tell me you're on the town council."

"No," Dixon said, "that I wouldn't do. Postmaster and rancher. That's it. And speaking of the ranch, I got to get back."

They both walked outside, stopped just in front.

"Try one of the other saloons," Dixon suggested. "You'll find a poker game."

"I'll give them a try," Clint said.

"My horse is behind the post office," Dixon said. "I'll see you tomorrow."

"Sure," Clint said, "I'll come by to mail a letter."

Dixon smiled. The two men shook hands and went their own way.

Across the street Al Wycliffe walked into the saloon, found Garver standing at the bar.

"You lookin' for me?" he asked.

"Yeah," Garver said. "Have a beer."

Wycliffe looked at the bartender and nodded. Little Jim wouldn't have moved otherwise.

"What's on your mind?"

"You got my message?"

"Yeah, I got it," Wycliffe said. "It didn't come at a very good time, but I got it. What's this about changing plans?"

"I had a visitor today," the lawman said. "A guest in our fair town."

"And who is that?"

"Clint Adams."

Wycliffe stopped with his beer halfway to his mouth.

"The Gunsmith is here?"

"That's right."

"Where is he?"

"Right now? I don't know. But in a couple of days he'll be gone."

"In a couple of days," Wycliffe said, "he'll be dead."

"Now wait," Garver said. "I didn't call you here to send you after the Gunsmith."

"You don't have to send me," Wycliffe said. "I'll go after him and kill him all on my own."

"You want to die that bad?" Garver asked.

"I want a rep that bad," Wycliffe said.

Garver turned and faced the larger man, showing no sign of backing down.

"Hey, listen," he said. "You're workin' for me, which means you do what I tell you to do. That means you want to go after the Gunsmith, you do it on your own time."

"What if I do that?" Wycliffe asked. "You can get somebody to replace me."

Garver slapped Wycliffe on his broad chest.

"Look, Al, this is too big, too important. I need you—alive."

"If it's so important, why you callin' it off, then?" Wycliffe asked.

"It's too dangerous with Adams in town."

"So I kill Adams, and it ain't dangerous anymore," Wycliffe said.

Little Jim was listening intently. Garver looked over at him, as if asking for support.

"It sounds good to me," Jim said. "If you want, I'll kill Adams for ya."

"No," Garver said, shaking his head. Then he looked at Wycliffe and repeated, "No. Nobody kills Adams. Okay, okay, we'll go ahead with the plan."

"Really?" Jim asked. "We're goin' ahead?"

"Yeah."

"And nobody will know?" Little Jim asked. "I won't have to give up my place?"

"I don't know why you'd want to keep this place," Garver said, "but no, you won't have to give it up."

"Good."

"So when do we go?" Wycliffe asked.

"I'll let you know," Garver said, "but it'll be soon. I just have to talk to a guy tomorrow."

Wycliffe pushed his empty mug over to Little Jim and said, "Gimme another one."

"You, Sheriff?" Jim asked.

"No," Garver said, "not me. I've got something to do."

Little Jim drew Wycliffe another beer and pushed it over to him.

Garver walked to the end of the bar and signaled for Jim to come over.

"What?" Jim asked.

"Under no circumstances," the lawman said, "are you to let him go and try to kill Clint Adams."

"I'll do my best."

"Do better than that."

"Where is Adams stayin'?"

"Why?"

"I need to know what hotel to keep Al away from."

"Keep him away from the Stetson."

"Like I said," Jim replied, "I'll do my best."

EIGHT

As Billy Dixon left town and headed for his ranch, Clint walked into the Tumbleweed Saloon. The young bartender saw him and waved him over.

"You interested in—" the man started, but Clint cut him off.

"I'm interested in a beer," he said. "That's it."

"Comin' up."

The bartender put a cold one down in front of him and waited.

"That's it," Clint said.

"That's all?"

Clint looked around, saw the gaming tables and the girls working the floor.

"It looks to me like I'll be able to find anything else I want in here," he said.

"That's for sure," the bartender said.

"Then I'll call you when I'm ready for another beer," Clint said.

"Okay," the bartender said, moving away.

As Clint turned to look the place over some more, the batwings opened and Sheriff Garver came walking in. He stopped just inside, looked around, spotted Clint, and came over to him.

"Mr. Adams."

"Sheriff," Clint said. "Can I buy you a beer?"

"Sure, why not?" Garver said. "I don't usually drink here, but I was doing my rounds, and saw you here, so I thought I'd stop in."

The bartender brought the sheriff a beer.

"Don't usually see you drinkin' in here, Sheriff."

Garver looked at the young man and said, "Go away."

The bartender obeyed.

Garver picked up his beer and looked at Clint.

"How was your visit with our postmaster?"

"Fine," Clint said. "We did some catching up."

"That mean you're leavin'?"

"No," Clint said, "we still have more catching up to do."

"So you're stayin' at his ranch?"

"No again," Clint said. "I have a room at the Stetson. You're sure in a hurry to have me leave town, Sheriff."

"I'm just thinkin' about my town, Mr. Adams," Garver said. "I don't want any trouble."

"Neither do I."

"You'll forgive me, but I don't think you always have a choice, do you?"

"You're probably right, Sheriff," Clint said. "Let me ask you something."

"Sure, go ahead."

"How'd you come to be sheriff of this town?"

"Every town deserves a good sheriff, don't you think?" Garver asked.

"And you're a good sheriff?"

"I like to think so."

"Why do I get the feeling you're not as uneducated as you like people to think?"

Garver smiled.

"What makes you say that?"

"Every once in a while you sound educated," Clint said. "It slips through."

"Does it?" Garver said. "I guess I'll have to watch that."

"Was it the act that got you voted in?"

"Probably," Garver said. "That's why I'll have to watch it." He put his empty mug down on the bar. "Thanks for the beer."

NINE

After Garver left Little Jim's, Wycliffe leaned on the bar and said, "Have a beer with me, Jim."

"Sure."

Jim drew two beers and brought them over to where Wycliffe was standing. There were about half a dozen other drinkers in the place by this time, but none of them were standing at the bar.

"Whataya think of Garver's plan?" Wycliffe asked.

"Sounds good to me," Little Jim said. "You got a problem with it?"

"I didn't," Wycliffe said, "until I heard that Adams was in town."

"You wanna go after him bad, don't ya?" Jim asked.

"Real bad."

"Well, seems to me," Jim said, "if we pull this job with the Gunsmith in town, he's liable to get himself involved. In which case—"

"I get my shot at him after all."

"Right."

Wycliffe nodded.

"They should call you Smart Jim."

"Yeah," Little Jim said, "they should."

They sipped some beer.

"You gonna do it alone?" Jim asked.

"What?" Wycliffe said.

"The Gunsmith," Jim said. "Are you gonna kill him alone?"

"Why?" Wycliffe asked. "You want to be in on it?"

"A chance to kill the Gunsmith?" Jim asked. "Who wouldn't be interested in that?"

"A lot of men wouldn't want any part of him," Wycliffe pointed out. "I think our sheriff is a man like that."

"You think Garver's afraid of Adams?"

"I think Garver's smart," Wycliffe said. "Smart men are always afraid."

"Why?" Jim asked.

"Because they're smart enough to be afraid," Wycliffe said.

"And you and me?"

Wycliffe grinned. "We ain't smart enough to let fear get in our way, Jim," he said. "That's why men like you and me, we usually do what we want and we don't worry about paying the price."

Jim nodded and asked, "How about some whiskey?" He reached behind the bar and picked up a bottle.

Wycliffe grinned and took it from him.

Clint read for a while in his room before deciding it was time to turn in. He got up off the bed, turned down the gas lamp on the wall, then walked to the window. Just for a moment he thought he saw two men in the street, but when he looked again, there was no one there.

Bad enough there were often men in the shadows, watching him. If he started to imagine them, he was done for.

He went to bed.

Jim grabbed the whiskey bottle from Wycliffe and pulled him out of the street.

"You don't want him to see you," Jim said.

"Why not?" Wycliffe asked.

"Because the time and place must be left to us," Jim said. "And when the time comes, we have to be sober."

"But the time is not now, is it?" Wycliffe asked.

"No," Jim conceded. "Not now."

"Then gimme back the bottle!"

TEN

Clint awoke the next morning, still thinking about the shadowy figures he'd seen on the street the night before. It was not like him to imagine such a thing, and he hadn't drunk enough for it to affect his perception.

After he washed up and dressed, he walked to the window and looked out. There were people crossing the street, walking on both sides, but no one seemed to be standing and watching the hotel with any interest.

He strapped on his gun and went downstairs to find some breakfast. He considered stopping at the post office to see if Dixon would be interested, but as postmaster, he probably would have reported to work early, and wouldn't be able to leave.

Clint went out onto the street, decided to go and find the place where he'd had the pie the day before. It seemed like a likely place to get breakfast. Also, he wanted to walk awhile to see if he could spot anybody following him this morning.

He arrived at the café without noticing any kind of a tail. There were plenty of tables so he was able to secure one in the back, against the wall and away from the windows. He ordered steak and eggs and remained alert while eating it. No one stopped in front of the café to peer in the windows. The coffee was not strong enough, so he made do with one pot, then paid his bill and left.

He stopped just outside the door and looked around. No one seemed to be paying any special attention to him, but he still refused to admit he might have been imagining things the night before. Perhaps whoever had been watching him then simply had something else to do during the day.

He decided to stop by the post office and bounce some questions off the postmaster while he did his job.

Billy Dixon had a small breakfast at home that he fixed himself, then spoke briefly with his foreman, Joe Kelly. Besides Kelly, he had three other employees, all ranch hands. Dixon had an idea that he might someday have a herd of decent horses, but at the moment there were about half a dozen ponies in the corral.

"There's a small herd of wild mustangs about ten miles south, in Central Valley, so I thought me and the boys would go and take a look," Kelly said.

"Leave one behind to watch over those six," Dixon said.

"Right."

"Joe, were you here yesterday when I got a visitor?"

"You mean Clint Adams?"

"So you were here."

"Yeah, I talked to him. I told him you was in town. Did I do somethin' wrong?"

"No, no," Dixon said. The foreman was about his age, but lacked Dixon's life experience. He had spent most of his life on one ranch or another.

"Did you tell anyone that the Gunsmith was here?" he asked.

"I guess I mentioned it to the boys."

"And did any of the boys go into town?"

"Nope," Kelly said, "I told them nobody goes to town until the weekend."

"Okay," Dixon said, "I don't want anybody talkin' about Clint Adams. Got that?"

"I'll let them know, boss."

"You do that," Dixon said. "Tell 'em I don't take kindly to anybody gossipin'."

"I'll tell 'em."

"Okay," Dixon said. "See what you can find out about them mustangs."

"I bet we'll have some of them in the corral when you get back."

"I'm lookin' forward to that."

When Clint entered the post office, the counter was empty and Dixon was nowhere in sight. Then he heard some noise in the back and walked to the rear. He found Dixon lugging a heavy burlap bag and rushed to help him.

"Looks like you need at least one more person here," he said as they hauled the sack to the front.

"Yeah, tell the town council that. They claim there's no more money." He straightened and rubbed his lower back. "Thanks."

"No problem."

"You wouldn't think a bunch of letters would be so damn heavy."

"I'm thinking if your back's hurting you, it's got a lot more to do with working your ranch than the post office."

"You're probably right." Dixon stepped behind the counter. "What's on your mind this mornin'?"

"I had the feelin' somebody was watching my hotel last night," Clint said.

"Like who?"

"Two men," Clint said. "Saw them standing in the street, kind of convinced myself I was imagining it."

"That wouldn't be like you."

"No, it wouldn't," Clint said. "I decided this morning they were there. Now I just need to figure out who it was."

"Anybody followin' you this mornin'?"

"No, I checked," Clint said.

"Well, let me know if you need anybody to watch your back."

"Your gun at home?"

"My gun and holster's home," Dixon said, "but I keep a Winchester right here." He picked the rifle up from behind the counter.

"Okay," Clint said, "I'll keep that in mind."

"Watch yerself," Dixon said. "Don't hesitate to call on me if you need to."

"I'll remember."

"I take an hour for lunch around one," Dixon said. "Come and join me."

"I will."

ELEVEN

Sheriff Garver was at the bank, in a meeting with the manager, Harold Birzer.

"Do you have enough guards?" Birzer asked nervously. He mopped his face with a handkerchief, even though it wasn't particularly warm in his office.

"I don't wanna have too many," Garver said. "Don't want to give ourselves away that somethin' big is goin' on. But don't worry, I've got good men."

"So then you're ready?"

"I think we're ready, Mr. Birzer," Garver said. "Send your telegram and have your money delivered."

Birzer nodded, then said, "Will you come to the telegraph office with me?"

Garver wanted to ask the bank manager what he thought anyone might steal from him as he went to and from the telegraph office, but instead he said, "Of course, Mr. Birzer."

"Thank you," Birzer said. "I'm very nervous about this."

"I can see that, sir," Garver said. "After you?"

Clint came out of the post office and saw Sheriff Garver walking on the other side of the street with a nervous-looking man in a suit.

"Hey, Billy."

Dixon came around the counter and joined Clint at the door.

"Yeah?"

"Who's that walking with the sheriff?"

"That's Harold Birzer. He's the manager of the bank," Dixon answered.

"The bank manager?" Clint asked. "How many banks in town?"

"Just the one."

"What do you know about Birzer?"

"He's always nervous, always sweatin'," Dixon said. "He thinks everybody who walks into the bank wants to rob it."

"Sounds like he's got the wrong job," Clint said.

"Or he's the right man for the job," Dixon said. "Far as I know, the bank has never been robbed."

"I wonder where they're going," Clint said.

"Could be anywhere," Dixon said. "Telegraph office is in that direction, but maybe they're just goin' to get coffee together."

"Think I'll tag along on this side of the street," Clint said. "I'll see you later."

"Yeah," Dixon said, "let me know what you find out, huh?"

"Sure."

Dixon went back inside while Clint started walking, keeping the sheriff and the bank manager in mind. They passed a saloon and a café without pausing, finally came to the telegraph office, and went inside.

He wondered what was going on only because Dixon had told him the lawman was crooked. Why was the crooked lawman walking with the bank manager? Was he also crooked? Were they planning something? Well, if the sheriff and the bank manager were planning on robbing the bank, that was their business. Clint was only supposed to be in town for a few days visiting Dixon. Why should he even care?

The answer was simple.

He had a hard time minding his own business when he knew a crime was about to be committed.

TWELVE

Clint found a post to lean against as he waited for the sheriff and the bank manager to come out of the telegraph office. At the same time he took a casual look around to see if anyone was watching him. No one seemed to be paying him any special attention. He still refused to believe, though, that he'd imagined the two men watching his hotel the night before.

He hated to think that he was starting to see things that weren't there.

While Bank Manager Birzer sent his telegram, Sheriff Garver looked out the front window and saw something he didn't like. Clint Adams was across the street, leaning against a post. He seemed to be watching the door of the telegraph office. Had he been standing there the whole time, or had he—for some reason—followed them there?

"Sheriff?"

Garver turned, realizing that Birzer was speaking to him.

"It's done," the bank manager said. "Is something wrong?"

"No," Garver said, "you'll just have to make your way back to the bank yourself, Mr. Birzer. I've got somethin' I need to take care of."

"Oh, well, all right," Birzer said. "I, uh, suppose I can do that."

"Yeah, you can," Garver said. "Nobody's gonna bother you."

"Well," Birzer said, "I hope not."

The two men walked out together, and Garver slapped the bank manager on the back.

"Go ahead," Garver said.

The bank manager nodded and headed back to the bank. Garver looked across at Clint Adams to see if he'd follow Birzer. He didn't. He remained where he was, looking at Garver. The sheriff considered walking across and asking Adams what was on his mind, but instead he turned and walked in the opposite direction from the bank manager.

Clint watched the bank manager walk back toward the bank. The sheriff stayed where he was, looking across at Clint. Clint had considered ducking inside to avoid the man, but he was standing in front of a hat shop. He would have looked more suspicious if he'd gone in there. So instead he stayed where he was and stared back, decided to see what would happen. After all, he was just killing time.

Abruptly, Sheriff Garver turned and walked away from the bank manager. Clint decided to keep pace, staying across the street, and see what occurred.

* * *

Garver saw that Clint Adams was following him—or at least, was keeping pace with him.

What did the man have on his mind?

The sheriff came to Little Jim's, stopped, thought a moment, then went inside. Let's see, he thought, if the Gunsmith is curious enough to follow me.

When Garver went into the saloon, Clint stopped, found another post, and leaned against it. He had two choices. He could stand there and wait, or go in and have a beer. Maybe the lawman would tell him something.

Yeah, he decided he could use a beer.

"What's goin' on, Sheriff?" Jim asked. "Little early for you, innit?"

"I'll have a beer, Jim," Garver said, "and one for my friend."

"Your friend?"

"Clint Adams," Garver said, "should be followin' me in here any minute."

"The Gunsmith?" Jim asked. "He's comin' in here?" He put his hand beneath the bar to check that his shotgun was still there.

"Don't get excited," Garver said. "Leave the shotgun where it is."

Jim pulled his hand away.

"Just wanted to make sure it was still there."

"Come on," Garver said, "two beers, before my new friend gets here."

"Comin' up."

THIRTEEN

Clint walked into the saloon, which had a small, almost invisible sign on it that said, LITTLE JIM'S SALOON. The sheriff was standing at the bar, and there were only a few other men in the place, seated at tables. Little Jim's was a bit smaller than the Big Tap, but the ambience was along the same lines.

The sheriff kept his back to the door, but he knew Clint was there. He was leaning over a beer mug. The bartender— a small man with a mean look on his face—watched as Clint approached the bar. When he got there, he saw the second beer.

"Sheriff."

"Your beer's gettin' warm."

Clint picked it up and drank from it.

"How'd you know I'd come in?" he asked.

"Why would you stand outside once you knew I saw you?" Garver asked.

"Thanks for the beer," Clint said, drinking from it again.

"Sure," Garver said. "What's on your mind?"

"What makes you think something's on my mind?"

"Well, you followed me and the bank manager to the telegraph office, and then you followed me here."

"Would you believe curiosity?"

Garver half turned toward Clint and leaned an elbow on the bar.

"You know, I would believe that," he said. "You know why?"

"No, why?"

"Because I can't think of any other reason you'd follow me."

"Boredom?"

"That, too," Garver said, "but boredom can get you into trouble, Adams. You know that better than anybody."

"You're right, I do," Clint said. "So I'll apologize. I was out walking, saw you and the bank manager, and for want of something else to do, I followed you."

"And you ended up gettin' a free beer out of the deal."

"Not bad," Clint said.

"Not bad at all," Garver said. He turned to the bar again, finished his beer, and set the empty mug down.

"I've got work to do," he said to Clint. "I'd appreciate it if you didn't follow me anymore."

"I'll try to find some other way of relieving my boredom," Clint promised.

"Good."

Garver left Clint with a half a glass of beer.

"You mind topping that off and making it colder?" he asked the bartender.

"I'll just get you a fresh one," the man said.

"Thanks."

Jim brought him a full mug of beer.

"Are you Jim?"

"Little Jim," the man said. "That's me."

"You don't mind being called 'Little Jim'?"

"Why would I?"

All the short men Clint had encountered in the past hated being referred to as "Little."

"I'm five foot one," Jim went on. "What else would you call me?"

"Big Jim?" Clint asked.

Jim laughed.

"That would be funny," he said. "I never thought of that."

"Have you been in town long?" Clint asked.

"A couple of years," Jim said, "since I opened this place."

"Have you known the sheriff all that time?"

"I've known Garver all that time, but he's only been sheriff the last few months. Why?"

"No reason," Clint said. "Like I told the sheriff, I'm just curious."

Clint drank down half his beer and then said, "Thanks for the beer, Jim."

"Big Jim," Jim said again, chuckling as Clint went out the batwing doors.

Sheriff Garver took up position inside one of the buildings across from Little Jim's, rather than standing out in the open the way Clint Adams had. He waited for Adams to leave, then watched as the man walked away in the direction of his hotel. He'd stayed in the saloon for a few minutes. Having another beer? the sheriff wondered. Or asking some questions?

He slipped out of the building by a side door and crossed the street to go back into Little Jim's and ask.

FOURTEEN

"He didn't ask anythin' about me?" Garver said to Little Jim.

"No," Jim said, "he asked about me."

"What?" Garver said. "What did he ask?"

"Well, he wanted to know how long I been in town," Jim said.

"And?"

"I tol' him two years, since I opened up this place."

"Yeah, yeah, but what else?" Garver said.

"Well"—Jim thought—"he wanted to know if I knew the sheriff all that time."

"That's it?"

"Well, yeah."

Garver frowned.

"What did you think he'd ask?" Jim said.

"I thought he'd ask some more questions about me," Garver said. "I thought I'd find out what was on his mind."

"Sorry," Jim said, "but that was it. Oh, I tol' him one more thing."

"What?"

"Well, when I told him I been here two years, and he asked me if I knew the sheriff all that time, I tol' him I knew you all that time, but you wasn't the sheriff the whole time."

"And that's all? Nothin' else?"

"Nope, that's it."

"Okay. Let me know if he comes in again."

"Okay."

As Garver started for the door, Little Jim called out, "Hey, Sheriff?"

"Yeah?"

"Whatayou think of me changing the name of this place to Big Jim's Saloon?"

Garver stared at Jim, frowned, and asked, "Now, why would you do that?"

"Well," Jim said, "see, I'm little, but if I called it Big—"

"That's not a good idea, Jim," Garver said. "It would just confuse your customers."

"Yeah, okay," Jim said, looking disappointed, "I guess you're right."

"I'm always right, Jim," Garver said. "Remember that, huh?"

As Garver walked out, Jim rubbed his jaw, cocked his head, and said, "Big Jim." It sounded okay to him.

Clint was waiting outside the post office when Billy Dixon came out and locked the door.

"What do people do for their mail while you have lunch?" he asked.

"They wait," Dixon said. "A man's gotta eat. You mind the same place?"

"No," Clint said, "it's fine with me."

When they were seated, Clint asked Dixon about his ranch. His friend told him how he wanted to raise horses, and how he was off to a small start.

"Well," Clint said, "you sure know horses."

"That I do."

"I met your foreman. Is he a good man?"

"He's okay," Dixon said. "And I've got three hands. They're out collecting some wild mustangs today."

"That sounds like fun."

"You want me to put you to work while you're here?" Dixon asked. "I could always use another hand—especially somebody as experienced as you."

"How would your foreman feel?"

Dixon shrugged. "Why would he object? He's still the foreman. I'm just givin' him an extra hand."

"You know," Clint said, "that does sound like fun."

"Good," Dixon said. "Be at my place tomorrow morning, first thing. I'm sure they'll be goin' out again."

"Okay."

"I'll even pay you a day's wages."

"I don't need a day's wages, Billy," Clint said. "Not from you."

"Well then, I'll buy lunch. How about that?"

"That's a deal," Clint said.

"Saw the sheriff and the bank manager go to the telegraph office today," Clint said.

"To do what?"

"I don't know. They went in, then came out and split up."

"Garver see you followin' him?"

"Yeah, he did. And we talked, in a place called Little Jim's."

"Little Jim," Dixon said. "There's a stone-eyed killer if there ever was one."

"Really?" Clint asked. "He looked kind of scruffy and harmless."

"Until he gets riled," Dixon said. "No, he's a killer, all right, with no remorse. He only keeps that place to give him somethin' to do between killin'."

"That's an odd person for a lawman to be associating with," Clint said.

"I tol' you, Garver's dirty. If you saw him with the bank manager, then somethin's goin' on with the bank."

"You think the sheriff is going to rob the bank?" Clint asked.

"I don't know," Dixon said. "It ain't my job to know. I keep my nose out of other people's business."

"That's something I've never been able to do," Clint said.

"Well, if Garver already knows that you were watchin' him, it's a little too late for you to start now. I'd watch my back if I was you."

"Maybe it's a good idea I'll be out at your place tomorrow."

"Sounds good," Dixon said. "Maybe they'll rob the bank and be gone by the time you get back."

FIFTEEN

Garver figured if Wycliffe wasn't at Little Jim's, he'd be with his favorite whore. He found her room and banged on the door.

Inside the room Patty was riding Wycliffe, his stiff penis stuffed all the way up inside her. Her head was back, exposing her long, smooth neck, and her eyes were practically rolled up inside her head.

Wycliffe's hands were on her tiny breasts, thumbing the brown nipples. The wide aureoles reminded him of fried eggs.

She was starting to gasp as her time approached, and then there was a knock on the door. Actually, it was more of a banging.

"No!" Patty yelled. She opened her eyes and glared down at him. "Don't you dare!"

"Come on, then!" he said, grabbing her hips. "Finish up."

"Damn you!" she said. She pressed her hands down flat

on his chest and began to ride him harder, looking for her relief, but now she was distracted.

"Ahhh!" she screamed, and climbed off him as the banging started again. "See who it is, damn it!"

Wycliffe had been very near his own completion, and as he got off the bed and stalked to the door, his penis was well out in front of him—long, and hard, and throbbing.

When he opened the door, the man outside jumped back.

"Watch that thing!" Garver said, stepping back as Wycliffe opened the door. "You could poke somebody's eyes out!"

"Garver," Wycliffe said, "what the hell."

"I wanted to talk, but are you busy?" Garver looked past him at the naked, angry whore on the bed.

"Look," Wycliffe said, "give me ten minutes—"

"Oooh!" Patty growled.

"Okay," Wycliffe amended, "a half hour and then I'll meet you at Little Jim's."

"Yeah, okay," Garver said, "but try to make it twenty minutes, will you?"

He looked down at Wycliffe's erection, rolled his eyes, and walked away. He hoped the man wouldn't catch it in the door when he closed it.

"Back already?" Jim asked as Garver entered.

"Waitin' for Wycliffe," he said.

"He with Patty?"

Garver nodded. Jim put a beer in front of him.

"Okay then," Jim said, leaning his elbows on the bar, "while you're here, let's discuss this Big Jim idea."

Garver nodded wearily, lifted his beer to his mouth.

* * *

"You gotta keep yer friends from bangin' on the door when we're fuckin', Al," Patty complained.

"I'll do my best."

She was lying on her back, catching her breath, sated now and not so mad. It had taken him twenty-five minutes to take her where she wanted to go.

"Come back when you're done," she said.

"More?" he asked.

She smiled at him.

"I got the day off from Miss Lily's."

Wycliffe nodded and said, "I'll be back."

What else was there to do in this town but eat, drink, and fuck until Garver's plan was ready?

SIXTEEN

Clint walked Dixon back to the post office, waited while the man unlocked the door.

"I got some whiskey inside," Dixon said.

"No," Clint said, "not for me."

"What you gonna do with the rest of your day?" Dixon asked.

"I guess I'll find a poker game," Clint said.

"Why don't you come out to the ranch tonight and spend the night? That way you'll already be there come mornin', and ready to go find some mustangs."

"I'll think it over," Clint said. "If I decide to come out, I'll meet you here; otherwise go ahead and ride home without me."

"Okay, but I'll be leavin' right at five," Dixon said. "I'm gonna fix some supper and eat at my own table tonight."

"I'll keep that in mind," Clint said. "No matter what happens, I'll see you in the morning."

"Right. Good luck. You're gonna need it the way you play."

"I'm a lot better than I used to be in our buffalo hunting days."

Dixon opened the door, said, "You'd have to be," and ducked inside, slamming the door behind him.

When Wycliffe entered Little Jim's, both Jim and Garver turned to look at him. There was one other man at the bar holding a beer. Little Jim leaned over and said, "Sit down!"

The man immediately picked up his beer and moved to a table.

"Beer?" Jim asked Wycliffe.

"Yep."

Garver looked at the time.

"Thirty-five minutes?"

"I couldn't leave the girl unsatisfied, could I?" Wycliffe asked, accepting a beer from Jim.

"No, of course not," Garver said. "Never let it be said you didn't leave whores satisfied."

"Hey," Wycliffe said, lifting the beer, "whores are people, too."

"If you say so."

Wycliffe drank down half his beer.

"What's on your mind this time?" he asked Garver.

"Clint Adams was following me today."

"Why?" Wycliffe asked.

Garver shrugged and replied, "He said he was curious when he saw me walking down the street with the bank manager. Now, how do you think he knew that Harold Birzer was the bank manager?"

"He asked somebody?" Wycliffe said.

"Maybe," Garver said, "but why?"

"Maybe he really was curious," Jim said.

"What else is he doin' here?" Wycliffe asked.

"I don't know what he's doin' here," Garver said, "but I don't want him payin' too much attention to me."

"So what?" Wycliffe asked. "Now you want me to kill him?"

Garver thought it over for a moment, then said, "Maybe. First, I have to be sure. If he's gonna get in the way, then yes, I'll want him killed. The two of you could probably do it, but I'd advise that you get some help. So between the two of you, come up with a couple of other names, hmm? Because if it's got to be done, I want it done right the first time."

"When?" Jim asked.

"I'll let you know."

He turned and walked out.

Garver stopped just outside the batwing doors and took a deep breath. He didn't want to make the wrong decision, so he was going to have to think about this long and hard.

He decided to go ahead and start his rounds.

"Whataya think?" Wycliffe asked Jim.

Jim shrugged.

"One way or another we're gonna kill the Gunsmith," he said. "I don't mind lettin' Garver call it."

"Whataya think about needin' two other men?"

Again, Jim shrugged.

"I don't mind," he said. "After all, Garver's gonna be payin' the freight, right?"

"Right."

"Another beer?" Jim asked.

"Sure," Wycliffe said, pushing the empty mug over, "fill 'er up."

SEVENTEEN

Clint found a poker game in the Tumbleweed and spent the afternoon taking money from the locals. Not much, though, since it was just a way to spend the time.

He gave some thought to Dixon's offer of spending the night out at the ranch. It probably made sense, but he would have had to meet Dixon at the post office at five, and it was already five-thirty.

Players had come in and out of the game over the past three hours, but it made no difference. Clint kept winning three out of every four hands. Most of them took it in good spirits, but for about half an hour one of the players had been fuming and complaining not about losing, but about Clint constantly winning.

"It don't make sense," he said. "How can one man win so much?"

"You shoulda been here all afternoon like me," Sam Wilton said. He was the only player who was still there from the time Clint first sat down, and he didn't much care that he was losing. It was more important to him who he was losing to. He was a merchant in town who had taken the afternoon off to play poker with the Gunsmith. He didn't care what it cost him.

"Naw, naw," the other man said. He was wearing trail clothes with some dust on them, so Clint figured he'd ridden into town not too long ago. "It ain't natural. No man can be that lucky."

"I don't think it's luck, friend," Wilton said. "It's just that he's that good, and the rest of us can't play for shit."

The other two men at the table laughed, but the complainer didn't find it funny.

"Maybe you can't play for shit, none of you," he said, "but I know this game. And I know when someone's cheating."

It got very quiet then. They all knew the one thing you didn't want to say at a poker table was the word "cheating." And you sure didn't want to accuse anybody of it. And you sure as hell didn't want to accuse a man like Clint Adams of doing it.

"Now, ease up, friend," Wilton said. "Nobody here wants any trouble."

"Shut up, old man," the complainer said. "I ain't talkin' to you."

Wilton sat back and fell silent. He did not have a gun, and the complainer did.

"What's your name, friend?" Clint asked.

"I'm Johnny Crespo," the man said proudly.

"Well, Johnny," Clint said, "I think the best thing for you

to do is get up from the table and go to the bar. I'll buy you a beer and you can drink it and calm down."

"Look, Adams, I know who you are and I ain't impressed," Crespo said. "In case you didn't hear me, I'm Johnny Crespo."

"I heard."

"That don't mean nothin' to you?"

Clint actually looked at Crespo for the first time.

"Not a thing."

"Well then, you ain't from around here," Crespo said. "People around here know my name."

"Probably," Clint said, "because you're a bigmouth."

They had become the center of attention, and now that brought some laughs from the onlookers.

Crespo stood up so fast he shook the table and knocked over his chair. His hand hovered just over his gun.

"You makin' fun of me, Adams?" he demanded.

"That's exactly what I'm doing, Johnny," Clint said.

"You better stand up and go for your gun!"

"Not a good idea, John—"

"I ain't funnin' with ya!" Crespo shouted, his face turning red.

Clint stared at the younger man.

"You really want to die while you're still in your twenties, Johnny?"

"It ain't me is gonna die," Crespo said.

"Okay," Clint said, "let's test that out."

"Whataya mean?"

"Let's try something," Clint said. "I'm going to stand up. Don't get trigger happy."

Clint stood up, kept his right hand away from his gun.

"Somebody give Johnny a beer," Clint said. "A full mug."

"I don't wanna beer."

"Just go along with me on this, Johnny," Clint said.

One of the girls brought a full beer to Crespo.

"Take it in your left hand, Johnny, and just hold it."

Johnny did so.

"Now, sweetie, bring me one, will you?" he asked the girl.

"Sure, Mr. Adams."

She was a pretty little brunette with round, pale shoulders and an impressive bosom. She went to the bar, came back, and handed Clint a beer, which he held in his left hand.

"Okay," Clint said.

"What the hell—"

"Here's the deal," Clint said. "We see who can shoot the beer mug out of the other man's hand first. That'll show us who is faster, and what would've happened if we'd slapped leather for real."

Around the room people started taking bets.

"I'll let you move first, Johnny."

Crespo licked his lips. The beer in his left hand shook a bit, spilling some on the floor. Clint's beer was as still as stone.

Suddenly, Crespo went for his gun, but before he could clear leather, the beer mug in his left hand shattered. Clint's bullet kept going and broke some glasses behind the bar, but the bartender had moved aside to safety.

Clint sipped from his beer, which still had not spilled a drop.

"Too bad, Johnny," he said, holstering his gun. "You would have died of a bad case of the slows."

Some more laughter from the room, and Johnny Crespo turned and stormed out of the Tumbleweed Saloon.

EIGHTEEN

Clint had replaced the spent shells in his gun with live ones, cashed out of the poker game, and was standing at the bar with a beer when the sheriff showed up.

"I heard there was a shootin'," Garver said to Clint.

"That what you heard?"

"Anybody hurt?"

"Just a beer mug," Clint said.

"What?"

"You shoulda seen it, Sheriff . . ." the bartender said, and explained exactly what happened.

"Crespo, huh?" Garver said.

"You know him?" Clint asked.

"Yeah," Garver said, "he fancies himself a gunman. Maybe you cured him."

"I hope so," Clint said. "If not, he's going to find himself dead very soon."

"That's his problem," Garver said. "My problem is you."

"Me? Why am I a problem?"

"Somebody's already tried to push you into a fight," the lawman said. "It's gonna happen again."

"That's not what happened, at all," Clint said. "He was playing poker and he was a poor loser. If someone else at the table would have been winning, he probably would have killed him. They were lucky I was the one who was winning."

"Tell me somethin'," Garver said.

"What?"

"Why'd you do that thing with the beer mug?" Garver asked. "Why didn't you just kill him?"

"Contrary to what you might think, Sheriff," Clint said, "I'm not out to kill anyone. If I can avoid it, I do."

"Well," Garver said, "that's sure not your reputation."

"I can't help that," Clint said. "Whatever my reputation is, I don't try to live up to it. So you've got no reason to run me out of town."

"I'm not runnin' you out," Garver said. "I'm just sayin' . . . I'll be watchin'."

"If somebody does get killed," Clint said, "it's not going to be my fault. You can count on that."

"I'll hold you to that," the lawman said. "What are your plans for the rest of the evening?"

"Another beer, and then a good book," Clint said.

"I hope that's true."

Garver turned and left the saloon.

"Bartender," Clint said, "another beer."

"Comin' up."

As the bartender set the fresh beer in front of him, the cushy little brunette sidled up to him.

"Are you really gonna go to your room and cuddle up

with a book?" she asked, pressing her warm hip up against his.

"That's what I was thinking," he said, looking down at her. "Why, do you have a better idea?"

"I might," she said, wiggling her shoulders saucily, also making her breasts jiggle.

"What time do you finish here?" he asked.

"Late."

"Well," he said, "I'll be awake, reading, if you want to come over." He told her what room he was in.

"You're pretty sure of yourself," she said.

"That is your hip pressing against mine, right?" he asked.

She bumped him and said, "What do you think?"

"Then I'll see you later."

NINETEEN

Clint was lying on his bed, still dressed but minus his boots, reading when the knock came at the door. It was a little after 2 a.m. He set the book down, slid his gun from his holster, and walked to the door. He cracked the door enough for him to see the girl in the lobby, then opened it—still with caution.

"Hello," she said.

"Hi." He stuck his head out to look both ways.

"Did you think I was going to bring company?" she asked. "Another girl maybe?"

"I think you'll be girl enough for me," he said, backing away.

"You can bet on that," she said, entering the room.

Her perfume was heady, smelled as if it had been freshly applied. He closed the door, then walked to the bedpost and replaced his gun in its holster.

"Guess a man like you has to be careful, right?" she asked.

"Definitely," he said. "It's how I stay alive."

She approached him, put her hand against his crotch, and said, "Mmm, I think I'm going to be glad you stayed alive."

He looked down at her bulging cleavage while she undid his belt. She reached into his pants and wrapped her warm hand around his hard penis.

"Mmm," she said again. She fell to her knees and tugged his pants down around his ankles. His penis popped free and her eyes widened. She took it in both hands, inhaled a deep breath, and then wrapped her lips around it.

Clint closed his eyes as she slid him into her hot mouth. She reached around and grabbed his buttocks with both hands, kneaded them while she suckled him. She then moved one hand down to fondle his testicles.

"Okay," he said, reaching down for her. "Come up here."

He pulled her up to him and kissed her soundly, then spun her around and pushed her down on the bed.

"Hey!"

He kicked his pants and underwear away, then quickly removed his shirt and joined her, naked, on the bed.

He raised the hem of her dress above her waist, tugged off her undergarment, and buried his face in her hot crotch.

"Omigod!" she gasped as his tongue lapped at her.

She struggled to get out of her dress, lifting it over her head and discarding it, then reached down and held his head in place.

"Oooh, yeah," she said, "ooh . . ."

He slid his hands up over her ribs to cup her breasts and squeeze them, popping the nipples with his thumbs. Her breasts felt so heavy and good in his hands that he decided they were demanding more attention.

He gave her one last, long lick, then kissed his way up her body to her breasts. He bit and licked her nipples, continued to massage her breasts while she reached between them for his penis. She grabbed him and held him tightly, yanking on him every so often as he continued to work on her big breasts.

"You men," she said, "you just love tits, don't you?"

"I love these tits," he said with his face buried between them.

"And I love this," she said, tugging on his cock again. "I guess we're both lucky."

He concentrated on her breasts a bit longer, and then she became impatient.

"Oh, please," she said, pushing him, trying to turn him onto his back. "Come on, come on . . ."

He finally rolled onto his back and asked, "Is this how you want me?"

Joe Crespo stared at the hotel, and the few windows that were still lighted.

"Which room?" he asked his brother.

"How do I know?"

"Johnny," Joe asked, "how are we supposed to get revenge on the man for shamin' you if we don't know where he is?"

Johnny pointed and said, "He's in that hotel."

"You know," Joe said, "you might be three years older than me, but you're still dumber."

"Never mind that," Johnny said. "We'll just wait here for him to come out."

"In the mornin'? I got better things to do than stand here all night."

"What do you suggest?"

"The whore just went in," Joe said. "He's gonna be busy for a while. We just gotta find out what room he's in."

"And how do we do that?"

Joe shook his head and said, "We're gonna ask. Come on."

TWENTY

"What's your name?" Clint said.

"What?" She stopped with one leg in the air.

"I think before I let you mount me, I should know your name."

"Is that important to you?" she asked.

"I thought it would be important to you."

She finished throwing her leg over him, then lay down on him, pinning his penis beneath her.

"Do you want my real name, or my saloon girl name?" she asked.

"They're different?"

"Yes."

"Well," he asked, reaching up and grasping her breasts, "whose tit am I grabbing now?"

"Oh," she said, closing her eyes, "those belong to Delores."

She began to rub her crotch over him. The combination of the roughness of her pubic hair and the slickness of her juices made him even more excited.

"Wow," he said as she began rubbing faster, "who does that belong to?"

She leaned down, pressed her mouth to his ear, and said, "That's Amy."

She lifted her hips and slid down on him, taking his dick into Amy's pussy while rubbing Delores's tits in his face.

In the lobby Joe and Johnny Crespo woke up the hotel clerk, who was sleeping with his head down on the desk.

"Huh?" Joe showed him a dollar.

"We want to take a look at your register."

"I can't do th—"

Johnny showed him his gun.

"We wanna look at your register."

The clerk snatched the dollar from Joe's hand and said, "Sure."

He took the book from behind him and pushed it over to the Crespo brothers.

"Here," Joe said, pointing.

Johnny looked and saw that Clint Adams was in Room 11. He nodded.

"Okay," Joe said to the clerk. "Thanks."

He pushed Johnny across the lobby and out the front door.

"What are ya doin'?" Johnny demanded.

"We gotta have a plan," Joe said.

"I know," Johnny said, "I plan to kill Clint Adams."

"Didn't you learn nothin' from that beer mug?" his brother asked him.

"Okay, okay," Johnny said, "So what do you suggest?"

"Just listen," Joe said.

* * *

It was fascinating to watch Amy/Delores ride him. Her big breasts bounced up and down, her nipples bobbing around in front of him. And the look on her face, her eyes wide open, biting her lip, tossing her head around. She was completely taken over by the moment. If two men burst into the room at that moment and started shooting, he doubted she'd even notice.

Suddenly, there was a knock at the door.

He ignored it, still watching her, feeling his release building, like it was rushing up from his legs into his crotch . . .

"What if he don't answer," Johnny whispered.

"What are you talkin' about?" Joe asked. "Somebody knocks on your door, you answer it."

"He's got a whore in there."

"It don't matter," Joe said. "Who don't answer the door when somebody knocks?"

He knocked again, harder.

The knocking came again, harder this time, and still she kept riding him. He thought about answering it, but suddenly he exploded inside her, his back arching, lifting them both off the bed. She began to spasm on top of him, and he could feel her insides gripping and releasing him, milking him . . .

"What the hell—" Johnny said when they heard the cries from inside.

"Ah, fuck it," Johnny said. "Kick it in."

"Now?" his brother asked.

"Right now!"

TWENTY-ONE

As the door slammed open, Clint reacted instantly, and from reflex. He lifted the girl off him and dropped her on the other side of the bed, so she'd be protected. Then he grabbed his gun from the holster on the bedpost. By the time the two men burst into the room, he had his gun trained on the door.

As Joe and Johnny Crespo rushed into the room, they saw that their idea had not been such a good one, after all. But they had their guns in their hands, and there was only one way to react. They pulled their triggers.

The brothers' shots, fired in haste, sprayed the room. Clint calmly fired back, striking each brother in the chest, precisely in the heart. They both fell to the floor, dead.

The girl—Amy or Delores, whichever name she wanted to use—stuck her head up from behind the bed and said, "Is it over?"

"Let's just make sure," Clint said.

He rose from the bed and padded, naked, to the bodies.

He kicked their guns away, then leaned over and checked the bodies.

"They're dead."

She stood up and walked, also naked and unconcerned about it, to the bodies.

"The Crespo brothers," she said.

Clint recognized Johnny Crespo, the man who'd complained about being cheated at poker.

"He had a brother," he said.

"Yes."

"No one mentioned that."

She shrugged, making her breasts jiggle. "I guess nobody thought it would be important."

"It would have been useful to know," he said.

He walked to the door and looked out. Some people had come out of their rooms and were milling about in the hall, wondering what happened. He tried to close the door but the lock was broken. It wouldn't stay closed.

He turned to the girl and said, "You better get dressed. We're probably going to have company."

She grabbed her clothes and began putting them back on.

"I hope we can get another room," she said.

He paused in pulling on his pants and looked at her.

"Well," she said, "I wasn't finished, were you?"

As expected, Sheriff Garver appeared soon, making his way through the people in the hall.

"Back to your rooms, please," he called. "Go back to your rooms."

He checked the doors, saw the one that was ajar, and

stepped to it. When he opened it and saw Clint Adams, he wasn't surprised.

"More trouble," he said.

Clint looked at the sheriff as he entered.

"Same trouble," Clint said, "just double."

Garver looked down at the bodies.

"Ah, the Crespo boys," he said. "This is a continuation of the trouble you had at the poker table."

"Obviously," Clint said. "Nobody bothered to mention to me that he had a brother. Are there any more Crespo family members?"

"Not that I know of," Garver said. "I think you've wiped the family out."

"That wasn't my intention," Clint said.

Garver looked over at the girl, who was fully dressed and sitting on the edge of the bed with the bodies at her feet.

"Amy," he said.

"Sheriff."

"You wanna tell me what happened?" the lawman asked.

"They broke in shooting, and Clint shot them," she said.

"That's it?"

"That's it," she said with a shrug.

"And what were the two of you doin' at the time?" Garver asked.

She smiled and said, "Just talkin'."

Garver looked at Clint, who stared back.

"Okay," the lawman said, "I'll get some men to remove these bodies."

"No hurry in my account," Clint said, picking up all his

belongings, "I'm going to get another room." He turned to
the girl. "Amy?"

She got up from the bed and stepped into the hall with
Clint, then turned to the sheriff and said with a smile, "We
haven't finished our conversation."

TWENTY-TWO

Clint got a new room from the desk clerk, and he and Amy—the name they finally settled on—returned to what they were doing.

If anything, having two men shot dead at her feet seemed to fuel her passion even more. As soon as they got to the new room, she dropped her dress and tore at his clothes, pushed him down on the bed, and mounted him again. She rode him long and hard again and again, seemingly completely insatiable, until finally she seemed to tire herself out. She collapsed on him at one point, and they both fell asleep.

He awoke with her lying next to him, but on his left arm. The sun was streaming through the window, shining in his eyes but on her naked back. He pressed his hand flat to her smooth back and felt the warmth of the sun there.

Carefully, he eased his arm out from under her and then walked to the window to look down at the town. At least what had happened reaffirmed his suspicions from the night before—there *were* two men watching his room from the street that night. At least he didn't have to keep looking over his shoulder for them.

"Hey?"

He looked at the bed. She was propped up on one elbow. Her breasts made his mouth water, like two overripe melons.

"Come back to bed," she said, reaching out. "It's early."

"I know," he said. "I have to be somewhere."

"Really?"

"Yes, really."

"That's too bad."

"I promised a friend I'd help him out."

"Oh, well, then," she said, turning onto her back, "you better go." She tossed the sheet off so he could see her whole body.

Hurriedly, he got dressed.

"Doesn't it bother you that you saw two men killed last night?" he asked.

She laughed and asked, "Did it seem like it bothered me?"

"No," he said. "That's what I mean."

"Clint," she said, "where I work I see a lot of shooting."

"And do they all excite you like last night?"

"Well," she said, "that was a combination of the shooting, and you."

He strapped on his gun and grabbed his hat, then walked to the bed. He ran his hands over her body, down between her legs, and then kissed her while he probed with one finger, making her wet.

"You bastard," she whispered.

He slid his finger out of her and smelled it.

"I'll take you with me all day," he said.

"Hey," she said as he headed for the door.

"What?"

She propped herself up on both elbows this time.

"That was pretty sexy."

He smiled and said, "I'll see you tonight."

He left the hotel, walked to the livery, and saddled Eclipse, then headed out to Billy Dixon's ranch.

As he rode out of town, Garver stepped out into the open. He didn't know how long Adams would be out of town, but he found the fact that he was leaving this early encouraging.

Time to get things under way.

"You're late," Dixon said as he rode up.

"Yeah, well, I got . . . busy last night," Clint said.

"What happened?"

"Crespo and his brother kicked in my door and tried to kill me."

"What happened?"

"I killed them. Garver didn't like it. It just proved his point about me and trouble."

"Well," Dixon said, "you're out here now. My men went out about an hour ago. I told them you'd be joining them."

"What about you?" Clint asked.

"I have to open the post office."

"Can't people go one day without their mail?"

"Yes," Dixon said, "and according to the government, that would be Sunday. Let me get my horse. I can ride part-way with you."

He went into the barn and came out walking his horse. They rode a few miles together, and then Dixon pointed the way to the valley where the mustangs were.

"My foreman, Kelly, is out with the men. He's expecting you. If you stay around later, you can eat with us."

"Okay, then," Clint said. "See you later."

TWENTY-THREE

Clint found the foreman and two other men in Central Valley. The three riders saw him, reined in, and waited for him to reach them.

"Kelly," Clint said. He recognized him from their first meeting.

"Adams," Kelly said. "Glad to have you. This is Charlie and Ed."

"Boys."

"Pleased to meet you, Mr. Adams," Charlie said.

Ed just nodded.

"Mustangs are in that direction," Kelly said. "About a dozen. Any good with a rope?"

"I'm a little rusty," Clint said, "but instead of roping them, why not just collect them all."

All three men stared at him.

"I don't mean to interfere," Clint said. "It was just an idea. I mean, there are enough of us."

"All?" Charlie asked.

"Just . . . drive them back to your ranch."

Kelly looked at the other two men, who nodded.

"Yeah, we can give that a try," the foreman said.

They spent morning tracking the herd. When they found them, there were fifteen of them, led by a dappled gray.

"Okay," Kelly said, "there are more than we thought. You two come in from the other side. We should be able to drive them to the ranch."

"I'm going to see if I can drive the gray," Clint said. "They should follow him."

"Okay," Kelly said, "let's go."

It took some doing, but the four of them were eventually able to drive the small herd back to the ranch. Once or twice the gray got it into his head to go a different way, but Clint was able to put him back on the right track.

When they had them in the corral, Kelly came over to Clint and said, "It was that Arabian of yours. That gray followed him."

Clint had figured that out, eventually. Every time the gray tried to go off on his own, he brought Eclipse in close. The gray seemed to gravitate toward the Darley.

"Lucky for us," Clint said.

"Come inside," Kelly said. "The boss'll be back soon. We'll get the grub goin'."

"Okay. Let me put my horse in the barn."

"The boys can do that."

"No," Clint said, "he gets ornery with strangers. I'll take him."

* * *

Clint unsaddled Eclipse in the barn, rubbed the horse down, and gave him some feed.

"We did an honest day's work today, big boy," he said, affectionately stroking the horse's huge neck.

He walked back to the house, found Kelly at the stove. The other two men were out at the corral, checking out the mustangs. Clint noticed that it was six thirty.

"What time does Billy usually get home from the post office?" he asked.

"Normally about this time, or a little earlier. It's about an hour from town—less with a horse like yours."

"Something must be keeping him."

"I'll get the boys from the corral," Kelly said. "Grub's ready."

While Kelly was gone, Clint figured he'd do his part so he found the plates and forks and put them on the table. When the men walked in, they laughed, having become easier around Clint after a day's work. All except for the man named Bob, who had stayed behind the whole day.

"Never thought I'd see the Gunsmith settin' the table," Ed said.

"Somebody's got to do it," Clint said.

The men each grabbed their own plate and walked to the stove so Kelly could fill them. When that was done, Kelly filled his own plate and joined them at the table. There was a coffeepot on the table that they all partook of.

"Where's the boss?" Ed asked.

"Dunno," Kelly said. "Somethin' musta held him up."

"Not like him to be late when you make stew," Charlie said.

"He'll be along soon," Kelly said.

But he wasn't.

By 8 p.m. Clint said, "Something's wrong. I better ride back into town and see."

"It's gettin' dark," Ed said.

"That's okay," Clint said. "My horse will handle it."

"I'll come with you," Kelly said. "You three stay here, keep an eye on those mustangs."

Clint and Kelly went out to the barn and saddled their horses.

"Has he ever been this late before?" Clint asked.

"Naw," Kelly said. "He likes to get back as early as he can, maybe even get some work in."

"Okay," Clint said, "then something's definitely wrong."

They mounted up and Kelly touched his rifle. "I'm ready."

TWENTY-FOUR

They rode into Adobe Walls a little after 9:30 p.m. The street was quiet but there was noise coming from the saloons.

"The post office?" Kelly asked.

"Yeah, we better check there first," Clint said. "We'd look silly if he was there and we didn't look."

They rode to the post office, dismounted, and tried the door. It was locked. Clint knocked, knocked again, but there was no answer.

"Okay, now what?" Kelly asked.

"Sheriff's office."

They walked their horse over there. Again, Clint tried the door, found it locked, and knocked a few times, but to no avail.

They looked at each other.

"Saloon," Clint said.

"Which one?"

"The Tumbleweed," Clint replied. "Somebody there's got to know something."

They walked their horses again, tied them off outside, and entered. They approached the bar and, while there wasn't much room, managed to elbow their way in. The same young bartender was working, so Clint called him over.

"What can I getcha?" the young man asked.

"Some answers," Clint said. "You seen Billy Dixon today?"

The man looked startled.

"You mean you ain't heard?" he asked.

"Heard what?"

"We had us a robbery here today," the barman said. "The bank had a cash delivery comin' in today and it got took."

"What's that got to do with Billy Dixon?"

"Well, he tried to stop 'em and they shot him down."

"Is he dead?" Kelly asked.

"I don't think so."

"Whataya mean you don't think so?" Kelly asked.

"Well, they carried him off to the doctor's and I ain't heard nothin'."

Clint and Kelly exchanged a glance.

The next stop was the doctor's office.

They hurried out of the saloon.

Kelly knew where the office was. It was a few streets away so they mounted up and rode there. The shingle outside the door said: DOCTOR A. KENNEDY, M.D.

"Doc Kennedy's good people," Kelly said. "He's come out to the ranch a couple of times to treat one of our hands."

They tried the door and, for once, found one that wasn't locked.

"Hey, Doc?" Kelly shouted as they entered.

Clint saw that they were in the living room of a house. The doctor probably had his examination room someplace in the back.

Suddenly, a man appeared, coming out of a hallway. He was tall, with steel gray hair even though he didn't seem to be forty yet.

"Kelly, right?" he asked.

"That's right."

"So somebody notified you?"

"Nobody told us anythin', Doc," Kelly said. "We came to town looking for the boss and heard that he got shot."

"That's right," the doctor said. "There was a robbery at the bank, some shooting. Mr. Dixon came running out of the post office, and before he knew what was happening, he got shot, twice."

"How bad?" Clint asked.

"Doc, this is Clint Adams," Kelly said.

"Billy and I are old friends," Clint said.

"Well, one wound is not serious. He got hit in the shoulder. The other hit him in the stomach, and I'm trying to keep it from getting infected."

"So he's gonna be all right?" Kelly asked.

"I'll probably know more by tomorrow," the doctor said.

"How is he now?" Clint asked.

"He's asleep."

"Can we see him?" Kelly asked.

"I don't want you to wake him up."

"I just wanna take a look," Kelly said.

"Well, all right."

Kelly looked at Clint.

"You go ahead," Clint said. "I'll stay here with the doc."

"Okay."

"You know where the room is," the doctor said.

Kelly went up the hallway.

"What'd the sheriff say about this?" Clint asked the doc. "What's he doing about it?"

"You haven't heard?" the doc asked.

"Heard what?"

"Well, it was the sheriff who robbed the bank."

TWENTY-FIVE

"Say that again?" Clint asked.

"The sheriff robbed the bank."

"Did he shoot Billy?"

"Well," the doc said, "he had some men with him. One of them might've done it."

"Do you know who the other men were?"

"They wore masks."

"Then how do you know it was the sheriff?"

"For some reason his mask came off in the bank and he was recognized."

"Anybody hurt?"

"The bank manager was killed," the doc said, "and it was the sheriff who shot him. There were witnesses."

"How many men with him?"

"I'm not sure," Doc said, "I heard three, or four."

Kelly came back.

"He looks bad," he said. "Pale, and small."

"He's in bad shape," the doctor said, "but tomorrow may be better."

"Doc, there are no deputies in town?"

"No."

"So what's being done about this?"

"As far as I know, nothing."

"What's goin' on?" Kelly asked.

"Come on," Clint said, "I'll tell you on the way."

"On the way where?" Kelly asked as they went outside.

Clint stopped.

That was a good question.

The sheriff's office was locked, City Hall was closed, as was the bank.

"How do we find out what's goin' on?" Kelly asked.

"Must be somebody from the town council in a saloon," Clint said. "Maybe even the mayor."

"So we just check the saloons?"

Clint nodded, said, "And see what we can find out. Otherwise, we'll have to stay 'til morning and go to City Hall."

"I wanna know somethin' now!" Kelly said. "I sure didn't like seein' the boss lyin' there in the doc's office."

They tried the Tumbleweed again. The bartender was unable to point out anyone from the town council who might be there.

"The mayor definitely ain't here," he said. "He's a teetotaler, wouldn't be caught dead in a saloon."

"That's so?" Clint asked.

"We better check the other saloons," Kelly said.

"Wait a minute," Clint said, then turned back to the bartender. "You wouldn't happen to know where the mayor lives, would you?"

The bartender smiled.

Clint and Kelly rode to a residential section of town, where the bartender said the mayor had a big house.

"You can't miss it," he said. "It's the only two-story house in town."

He was right. It stood out among all the other small, one-story homes.

They rode right up to it, dismounted, and tied their horses off to a pole out front. They climbed the five stairs to the front door and knocked.

A large man with grease on his face and a napkin tied around his neck answered.

"What the hell—" he said. "We're eatin' our dinner."

"Are you the mayor?" Clint asked.

"That's right, Mayor Corby," the man said. "What do you—"

"Let's talk inside," Clint said. He put his hand against the man's chest and pushed him back into the house.

"What's goin' on—" he started to demand, but they followed him in and Kelly slammed the door.

"Dear, what's wrong?" a woman's voice called out. "Who is it?"

"That's my wife," the mayor said. "Don't hurt her."

"We're not here to hurt anyone, Mayor," Clint said. "We're here to talk about today's bank robbery. Just tell her you'll be there in a minute."

"I'll be there in—in a minute, love," the mayor called out. "It's just some . . . city business."

"Don't they know not to bother you at home?" she asked wearily.

"We'll make it fast," Clint said. "What's being done about the robbery?"

"Nothin' yet," the Mayor said. "I'm gonna send a telegram to the Texas Rangers tomorrow."

"And if they agree to come, how long will it take?" Clint asked.

"Probably three days to get here."

"That's not soon enough," Kelly said. "They'll be gone by then."

"Who are you men?"

"My name's Kelly," Kelly said. "I'm the foreman on Billy Dixon's ranch."

"Too bad about Dixon. How is he?"

"Still alive," Clint said.

"And you?"

"I'm Clint Adams."

The mayor's eyes widened.

"I heard you were in town, but I thought you left," he said.

"Well, I'm back. Look, you've got to send someone after those bank robbers."

"That's the problem with havin' your sheriff rob the bank," the mayor said. "You don't have anyone to send after 'em. Unless you . . ."

Clint stared back at the man for a few moments, then said, "Well, damn it, if there's no one else."

"I'll go with you," Kelly said. "The rest of the men will, too, if we have time to get them."

"Wait a minute," the mayor said, and disappeared into

his house. He returned a moment later, holding out the sheriff's badge.

"He left this at the bank. I had it in my pocket when I came home." He held it out to Clint. "You take it."

"Not me," Clint said. "Kelly, you take it."

The mayor held it out to the foreman.

"You'll need some official standing."

Kelly hesitated, then accepted the badge.

"Don't we need some words?" he asked.

"Consider yourself sworn in," the mayor said. "Here." He took the badge back and pinned it on the foreman's chest.

"We can get an early start in the morning," Clint said. "We won't be able to track them at night."

"The town appreciates this, men."

"Yeah, well," Clint said. "We're doing it for Billy Dixon."

"Whatever the reason," the mayor said, "come by my office in the morning and I'll give you a few deputies' badges, just in case you can recruit anyone."

"We'll see you in the morning, Mayor," Clint said. "Sorry we interrupted your supper."

"Think nothing of it."

Clint and Kelly left the house, stopped just outside the door. Kelly looked down at the badge on his chest.

"Sure didn't expect this when I woke up this morning," he said.

TWENTY-SIX

Clint and Kelly went back to the Tumbleweed.

"Hey," the bartender said, "looks like you made some progress." He drew two beers and set them down. "On the house . . . Sheriff."

"Is there anybody in here who works at the bank?" Clint asked.

"Lemme see." The man looked out over the sea of faces in the place.

"Or maybe just somebody who was in the bank when it was robbed?" Kelly asked. "Or outside of it?"

"I think I saw Andy Sawyer in here before," the bartender said. "He was telling folks how he was in the bank just minutes before the robbery, and that he saw everything from across the street."

"Okay," Clint said, "where is Sawyer?"

"Here comes Delores," the bartender said. "Ask her if she's seen him?"

Delores came over to the bar and settled herself between Clint and Kelly, leaning on Clint.

"I bet you're not here to see me," she said.

"We're looking for Andy Sawyer," Clint said.

She craned her neck and said, "I think I saw him sittin' near the back with some friends . . . yeah, there he is."

"Where?" Clint asked.

"All the way in the back, but red hair that kinda stands up on his head, like he was hit by lightning or somethin'."

Clint could see the shock of red hair from across the room.

"What's he drinking?" he asked.

"Whiskey."

"Bring him one on me," Clint said.

"He's got a bottle, but it's almost empty."

"Then bring him another one."

"Okay."

She turned to the bartender, who handed her a full bottle. Clint paid the man for it while she took it to Sawyer. When she handed it to him, she pointed to the bar, and Clint raised his beer mug. Sawyer grinned and accepted the bottle.

"Let's go," Clint said, "before he gets too drunk to talk."

"Just remember one thing when you talk to him," the bartender suggested.

"What's that?"

"Andy Sawyer is a big liar."

By the time they reached Sawyer, he already had the new bottle open. Clint grabbed it out of his hand.

"Hey!" Sawyer complained. "You just bought that for me."

"We need you to answer a few questions first," Clint said.

Kelly looked at the two men who were sitting with Sawyer and said, "Get lost."

They did.

"Hey, you scared my friends away!"

"So when I give you back the bottle," Clint said, "you won't have to share it with anybody."

Sawyer thought for a moment then a toothless grin spread over his freckled face and he said, "Hey, yeah!"

Clint and Kelly took the chairs Sawyer's two friends had just vacated.

"What's this all about?" Sawyer asked.

"The bank robbery today," Clint said. "You've been telling people you were in the bank moments before the robbery, and that you saw everything from across the street."

"I was," Sawyer said. "I did . . . I saw everything."

"You saw everything that happened outside the bank," Clint clarified.

"That's right."

"Tell us."

"Tell you what?"

"Everything you saw," Clint said. "Come on."

"Okay, okay," Sawyer said. "I came out of the bank and crossed the street. I went into Little Jim's but I couldn't get a drink because he wasn't there. I came back out and saw the men come running out of the bank—oh, after a couple of shots."

"That's when Garver shot the bank manager," Clint said. "Go ahead."

"Well, the men came runnin' out and got on their horses.

They started to ride out, and I saw the postmaster come out of the post office."

"Did he have a gun?" Kelly asked.

"He had a rifle."

"Okay," Clint said, "go ahead."

"The postmaster came out, looked around, but before he knew what was happening, they were on him. One of them shot him twice."

"What about the men?"

"What about them?"

"Well, how many of them were there?"

"Four."

"What did they look like?"

"They had masks on."

"Body types, then."

"I dunno," Sawyer said. "Kinda tall, I guess . . . wait, one of them was small."

"How small?" Clint asked.

"I dunno," Sawyer said. "Shorter than the others."

"Okay, so one was short, three were tall," Clint said. "Were they husky, thin . . . what?"

"Lemme think." Sawyer eyed the whiskey bottle. "Two . . . two of them were thin, one was thick."

"The thick one had to be the sheriff," Kelly said.

"Thin," Clint said, "two tall thin men, one short . . . was the short man thick or thin?"

"Thin," Sawyer said.

"Little Jim thin?" Clint asked.

"Yeah, maybe."

Clint gave Sawyer the bottle, turned to Kelly.

"One night I thought I saw two men outside my window. I think one was tall and thin, the other short."

"You think one was Little Jim?"

"A Little Jim type," Clint said, "but maybe . . . Billy told me that Little Jim is a killer, just runs the saloon for something to do."

"That's true enough," Kelly said.

"Garver drank there, so maybe they were friends."

"So the thick man was Garver, and the small man was Jim?" Kelly asked.

"It's possible," Clint said.

"So what do you want to do now?" Kelly asked.

"Let's go over to Little Jim's," Clint said. "Since his face was covered, maybe he'll go back there."

"You really think he would?"

"Sawyer said the front door was open and nobody was behind the bar," Clint said. "Maybe he left it open because he knew he'd be back."

"But leavin' it unlocked," Kelly said, "that leaves him open to havin' folks come in to drink for free."

"Well, supposedly he doesn't care," Clint said. "He's just running the place to have something to do."

Kelly shrugged then and said, "Well, it don't hurt to check."

TWENTY-SEVEN

They left their horses in front of the saloon and walked over to Little Jim's. Like Sawyer said, the front doors were wide open. They went in, found the place empty with nobody behind the bar.

"I thought there'd be some men in here drinkin' for free," Kelly said.

"Well, since folks seem to know that Little Jim's a killer, maybe that's as good as keeping the doors locked."

"You might be right."

"Let's see if there's an office, or a back door, or something."

They searched, found a small office with a rolltop desk. Clint went through the drawers, found one drawer filled with unpaid bills.

"He really doesn't care about this place," he said, closing the drawer. "He doesn't bother to pay his bills."

"Maybe his creditors are afraid of him, too."

They left the office and went back into the saloon. In the

back they found a store room, and a back door that was also unlocked.

"Whataya wanna do?" Kelly asked.

"There's nothing to do," Clint said, "so let's wait here awhile and see if he comes back."

Kelly eyed the bar and asked Clint, "Want a drink while we wait?"

Just outside of town Garver was hunkered down by a fire, waiting for the second pot of coffee to be ready. With him were Wycliffe and Little Jim and a man named Stanford, who was nervous.

"You sure a posse ain't out there lookin' for us?" he asked.

"I told you," Garver said. "I'm the sheriff—I was the sheriff—so there's nobody to get a posse together."

"Won't they just name a new sheriff?" the man asked.

"Believe me, Stanford," Garver said, "even if they do name a new sheriff, it'll take them days. Nobody in that town wants the job. Now why don't you go and stand watch?"

Stanford stood up, then asked, "If there ain't no posse, why are we standin' watch?"

"We're just being careful, Stanford," Garver said. "Now go."

As the man left, taking his rifle and a cup of coffee with him, Wycliffe asked, "What if Clint Adams takes that badge?"

"He wasn't even in town when we left," Garver said. "Even if he takes it, it'll be a while."

Little Jim dumped the remains of his coffee into the fire and stood up.

"I'm goin' back into town," he said.

"What for?" Wycliffe asked.

"I left my place open."

"Nobody's going to touch anything there," Garver said. "They're afraid of you."

"Don't matter," Jim said. "I gotta go. 'Sides, I'm changing the name."

"To what?" Wycliffe asked.

"Big Jim's."

"Ain't gonna work," Wycliffe said.

"Why not?" Jim asked.

"Nobody's gonna believe it."

"It's got . . . what's it got?" Jim asked Garver.

"Irony."

"Yeah," Jim said, "it's got irony."

"Here's your cut," Garver said, handing Jim some packs of cash. It took two hands to hold them.

"How much?" Jim asked.

"Thirty thousand."

Jim took the money and shoved it into his saddlebags.

"Don't start spending it too soon," Garver said.

"I don't spend my money," Jim said.

He saddled his horse while the other two watched him, then rode off with a wave.

"Why not kill him instead of lettin' him go back?" Wycliffe asked.

"You want to try and kill him?" Garver asked. "Be my guest."

"No, not me," Wycliffe said. "The little monster is a killin' machine."

"You answered your own question, then."

"Maybe I shoulda went with him," Wycliffe said.

"What for?"

"He might find himself goin' up against the Gunsmith," Wycliffe said, "since you shot the postmaster, Dixon."

"He was about to take some shots at us," Garver said. "He might have hit any of us. Seems to me I might have saved your life."

"Yeah, maybe," Wycliffe said, "but killin' the bank manager, that pretty much makes sure there'll be a posse after us eventually."

"Well, he recognized me. I had no choice. Besides, you know what they're gonna do?" Garver asked. "They're gonna track Little Jim right back to town."

"How they gonna do that?"

"When we break camp," Garver said, "we're gonna wipe our tracks out."

"But not Jim's?"

"Not Jim's."

"So that's why you didn't want to kill him," Wycliffe said. "It wasn't that you was afraid of him."

"No," Garver said, "I'm not afraid of the little monster."

"Yeah," Garver said with a shrug, "me neither."

Jim rode back to town, rode his horse right up to the back door of his place. He knew he'd taken a chance, leaving the front doors open, but he didn't want anyone questioning the fact that he was closed. Besides, Garver and Wycliffe were right. Nobody would have the nerve to drink his beer or booze while he was gone—not without leaving some money on the bar anyway.

He dismounted, shouldered his saddlebags, and went in the back door.

TWENTY-EIGHT

Little Jim went into his saloon and moved around behind the bar. He took the saddlebags off his shoulder and placed them on top of the bar.

Clint came out of the little office, and Kelly walked through the front door.

"Hey," Jim said to Kelly, "want a drink?"

"No drinks, Jim," Clint said.

Jim turned quickly and looked at Clint. Then he looked at Kelly and noticed the badge. Then looked at Clint again.

"What the hell—" he said. "What the hell were you doin' in my office?"

"Where've you been, Jim?" Clint said.

"What's it to you?"

"I got a better question," Kelly said. "What's in the saddlebags?"

Jim looked at Kelly.

"None of your business."

"I think we're going to make it our business, Little Jim," Clint said.

"Big Jim," the small man said. "I'm changin' my name to Big Jim."

Clint studied the man. He wasn't wearing a gun, and he wasn't carrying a rifle, yet he had been described as a killer.

"Little J—Big Jim," Clint said, "have you seen your friend Garver?"

Jim looked at Kelly.

"Why are you wearin' the sheriff's badge?" Jim asked.

"I'm the new sheriff."

"Since when?"

"Since you and Garver robbed the bank, and killed the bank manager."

"We're gonna have to take a look inside those saddlebags, Jim," Kelly said.

"Like hell," the little man said.

Kelly took one step toward him, and Jim reached under the bar. Clint knew he had a split second to make a decision. If he was too slow to act, Kelly would be dead.

Jim was coming out from under the bar with a shotgun when Clint drew. As if he sensed his danger was from Clint, the little killer turned toward him, ignoring Kelly. As Clint fired, Jim pulled both triggers on the shotgun. Both barrels discharged into the bar, splintering it. Clint's bullet went into Jim's chest, and he went down behind the bar.

Clint walked to the bar, checked Jim to determine that he was dead.

"He was pretty quick with that shotgun," Kelly said. "I didn't have time to react."

"Forget it," Clint said. He replaced the spent shell and holstered his gun. "Check the saddlebags."

Kelly opened the bags and found the cash.

"Jeez," he said. "I never seen this much money."

Clint spread the bank bundles out on top of the bar.

"Looks like thirty thousand," he said. "We should find out how much was taken from the bank."

"We'll have to wait 'til tomorrow, then," Clint said. "We'll have to talk to somebody at the bank before we go—or maybe the mayor will have the numbers."

"The mayor . . ." Kelly said, shaking his head. "What a waste."

"That's the way he seemed to me, but right now we have to deal with him."

"Okay. What do we do with the money for now?"

"I'll keep it in my room," Clint said. "And we should get you a room."

"What about him?" Kelly asked.

"Let's lock the front door and go out the back. Forget about him for now."

"As the law, I should do something about the body," Kelly said.

"Tomorrow we can have it taken over to the under-taker's."

"Okay."

"So let's get out of here now, before somebody comes to see what the shooting was all about."

Kelly moved quickly, slammed the front doors, and locked them. Then they walked through the back room and out the back door, Clint with the saddlebags. Little Jim's horse was still there, and they decided to just leave it there.

* * *

They went to the hotel and got Kelly a room right across from Clint's. On the second floor they stopped in front of their rooms.

"If either of us hears shots, we'll come running," Clint said.

"Okay."

Kelly's eyes went to the saddlebags.

"Something on your mind?" Clint asked.

"I just wondered . . . you ever think about keepin' that money?"

"No," Clint said.

Kelly hesitated, then said, "Me neither."

TWENTY-NINE

The night went by without incident. Clint knocked on Kelly's door, carrying the saddlebags, early the next morning.

"We need some breakfast," Clint said, "then we'll go and talk to the mayor."

"What about getting an early start?" Kelly asked.

"We found out something we needed to know last night," Clint said. "Now we have to tell the mayor about little Jim and get the body taken care of. And we have a good place to start tracking Garver and the rest."

"I'm not a tracker," Kelly said. "How will we do that?"

"Easy," Clint said. "We just track Little Jim back to where he came from—probably a camp. From that camp we can track Garver."

"You'll track him," Kelly pointed out. "I'll follow you."

"That'll work," Clint said. "Let's get something to eat."

* * * *

They stopped at a café and ate breakfast with the saddlebag of $30,000 on the floor between them. They both had steak and eggs, and Clint paid the bill from his own pocket.

"Don't you think the bank owes us a breakfast?" Kelly asked. "After all, we got some of their money back."

"That's okay," Clint said. "I can afford breakfast. Come on, we don't have a bank manager to return the money to, so we'll give it to the mayor."

"What if he keeps it?"

"That's not our problem," Clint said. "As long as we retrieve it and return it, I don't care what happens to it."

They left the café and walked to the City Hall.

Clint and Kelly were shown into the mayor's office by a middle-aged secretary.

"Ah, gentlemen," the mayor said, "I have the badges for you." He spread about half a dozen badges across his desk. Kelly picked one up and gave it to Clint.

"Thanks," Clint said, putting the badge in his shirt pocket. "Mayor, we'd like to know how much money was taken from the bank."

"A hundred and twenty thousand dollars was taken from the bank. That's the number I got."

Clint dropped the saddlebags on the mayor's desk.

"What's this?"

"Thirty thousand."

"What?"

The mayor opened the saddlebags and took out the bank packets.

"You got some of it back already?" he asked. "I put the badges on the right men obviously."

Clint let Kelly tell the mayor about Little Jim's involvement with the robbery, and what happened at his saloon.

"So he's dead in the saloon right now?" the mayor asked.

"That's right," Kelly said. "I need somebody to go and get him and take him to the undertaker's office."

"I can get somebody to do that," the mayor assured him. "What are you going to do?"

"Clint and I are going to follow Jim's trail and hope it leads us to the rest of the bank robbers."

"I want you to know," the mayor said, "that as long as you bring the rest of the money back, I don't care how you bring Garver and them back."

"Are you sayin' dead or alive?" Kelly asked.

"That's what I'm saying, gents," the mayor said. "Dead or alive."

When they left the mayor's office, they went right to the livery for their horses.

"It's obvious we're looking for Garver," Clint said while they were saddling their mounts. "I don't think we need to ask any more questions."

"Too bad we couldn't find out from Jim who else was involved."

"We didn't have much choice in that," Clint said. "We'll find out when we catch up to them."

They walked the horses outside.

"What do you think about the mayor sayin' he wanted Garver and his men dead or alive?"

"I think he's looking to avoid trying them, and he wants us to do his job for him. But I'd prefer to bring them in alive."

"And what about the boys at the ranch?" Kelly asked. "I've got all these badges in my saddlebags now."

"Let's see what direction Jim's trail takes us in," Clint said.

"Can we pick it up here?" Kelly asked.

"No," Clint said. "His horse is still behind his saloon. We'll pick it up there."

THIRTY

They went back to the saloon and went around to the rear, where Little Jim's horse was standing.

"Just give me a minute," Clint said, dismounting, "then we'll take this animal to the livery and go."

Clint went over to the horse, checked all four hooves for identifying marks, and then looked at the dirt in the alley.

"Okay," he said, "I've got it."

"Got what?"

"The tracks," Clint said. "I'll be able to pick them out and follow them."

Clint mounted up, then grabbed the reins of Little Jim's horse. They took the animal to the livery so it could be cared for, then went back to the saloon to pick up the tracks.

"Which way are they headin'?" Kelly asked.

"These tracks head south," Clint said.

"The direction of the ranch," Kelly said. "If we get that far, we can pick up the boys and deputize them."

"We'll have to see," Clint said. "I expect to follow these tracks to a camp. We'll have to see where the others went from there."

They rode through town, Clint following as well as he could, but when they got to the street, there were just too many tracks there.

"Let's go south of town and see if we can pick him up there."

South of town, Clint was able to pick up Little Jim's tracks again. Within a few hours, they found where Jim had camped the night before.

"That took a lot of nerve," Kelly said, "camping this close to town."

"That's because Garver knew there was no posse after them."

"Well," Kelly said, "when we get to the ranch, there will be a posse."

"Let's see if these other tracks head that way," Clint said.

"How many?"

"Three," Clint said, "just what we expected."

Clint dismounted and walked the cold campsite. He saw Little Jim's tracks trail off toward town. The other three tracks led off to the south. If they kept going that way, they would, eventually, come very near to Billy Dixon's ranch.

"Okay," Clint said, mounting up, "We'll follow and hope they don't veer off, or split up. If they split up, we may have to split up, too."

"I'm followin' you," Kelly said. "I may be wearin' the badge, but you're the leader."

"There's no leader," Clint said. "Let's just follow these tracks and see what happens."

"What's that?" Wycliffe asked. "Down there?"

"It's a ranch."

"Whose?"

Garver squinted, looked around to make sure they were where he thought they were.

"Oh," he said, then, "that's Billy Dixon's ranch."

"Dixon? The hero of Adobe Walls?"

"That was a while ago," Garver said. "Now he's just the postmaster in town."

"Think he'll be there?" Wycliffe asked.

Garver knew he'd already shot Dixon down in the street, so he said, "I doubt it."

"That corral's full of horses," Wycliffe said. "We could use some fresh mounts."

"You got a point," Garver said. "Okay, we go down and gets some mounts. From what I know of Dixon's ranch, there are only a few hands."

"What do we do with them?" Stanford asked.

"We kill them," Garver said. "Anybody got a problem with that?"

"I don't," Stanford said.

"Me neither," Wycliffe said. "But I got another question."

"What?" Garver said.

"Can you break a wild horse?"

"Why?"

"Those are wild mustangs," Wycliffe said, "but we're lucky. I can break 'em."

"Gotta be a few horses down there we can ride," Stanford said.

"Only one way to find out," Garver said.

"We kill 'em first thing?" Stanford asked, touching his rifle.

"Leave your rifle," Garver said. "We'll talk first, and shoot later."

THIRTY-ONE

Garver, Wycliffe, and Stanford rode down to the Dixon ranch. As they approached, the mustangs in the corral began to shift around nervously.

"You're right about those mustangs," Garver said. "They're wild."

"Might be some more horses in the barn," Wycliffe said.

"We'll take a look," Garver said. "First let's be sure how many men are here."

"There's one, comin' out of the barn," Stanford said.

"He'll be yours," Garver said, "but only when I say. Got it?"

"I got it," Stanford said.

"Here's mine," Wycliffe said.

A man wearing chaps came out from behind the corral.

"Good," Garver said.

The door to the bunkhouse opened and another man came out.

"That's three."

And they quickly determined there were no others.

Ed was behind the corral, looking the mustangs over, trying to decide which ones he should break first, when they got nervous. That was when he heard some men riding in. He came around the corral and saw them riding toward the house. He didn't have a gun on him.

When Bob heard the horses ride in, he came out of the barn to see what was happening. He had left his rifle inside.

Charlie came out of the bunkhouse to see who the riders were. He had thought to strap on his gun before he came out.

That was why he was the first to die.

"Okay, boys," Garver said. "Take your man."

Garber drew and shot down Charlie before the man could react.

Wycliffe turned his horse and very deliberately drew his gun and shot the man in the chaps.

The bullet struck Ed in the chest, punched all the air from his lungs even before he realized he'd been shot.

Stanford turned his horse, but his man—Bob—had turned and run back into the barn.

Stanford, unaware that Bob had a rifle in the barn, rode up to the open door of the barn, his rifle held lazily in his hand.

From inside, Bob waited for the man to appear, and when he did, he shot him.

The shot hit Stanford in the hip and knocked him off his horse.

Garver and Wycliffe turned and saw Stanford get shot from his saddle.

"Idiot," Garver said.

"I'll go around the back," Wycliffe said, and gigged his horse into motion.

Garver waited for Wycliffe to get around to the back, then rode his horse over to the barn and dismounted outside.

Stanford was lying on his side in the dirt, groaning.

"How bad, Stanford?" Garver called.

"It hurts," Stanford said.

Garver shook his head and shot Stanford in the back.

"Doesn't hurt anymore," he said.

Wycliffe rode around back and dismounted. Like most barns, there was space between the boards and he was able to peer inside. He saw a man with a rifle keeping his eyes on the front door.

He looked around, saw a regular-size door in the back, and moved to it.

"Hey, in the barn!" Garver said. "All we want is some horses."

"Corral's full of 'em," Bob said.

"Yeah, well, we'd like something that's already broke and ready to ride," Garver called. "Like what you got in there."

"I'll send 'em out."

"Good idea," Garver said.

"You want 'em saddled?"

"That's real nice of you, but we got our own saddles. Just send the horses out."

"How many?"

"Two will do."

Garver waited, gun drawn, and when he heard the sounds of the horses' hooves, he stepped out of hiding.

Wycliffe heard Garver and the man talking, waited for his chance.

The man inside got a couple of horses out of their stalls, aimed them at the front door, and slapped them on the rump.

That was when Wycliffe stepped through the door.

Both Garver and Wycliffe came in shooting. The bullets struck Bob from the back and the front. He did a little dance as the bullets struck him, then he fell to the ground, dead.

Garver approached the body, looked down, and nudged it with his boot.

"Dead?" Wycliffe asked.

"He is."

"How's Stanford?"

"Dead."

"Stupid," Wycliffe said, holstering his gun.

They looked around, saw there were three more horses in the barn. They wouldn't have to go out and chase the other two down.

"Let's bring in our horses and saddle two of these up," Garver said.

"What about the bodies?" Wycliffe asked.

"What about them?"

"We don't want anybody passin' by to see them," Wycliffe said.

"You're right," Garver said. "Let's bring all four of them in here before we do anything else."

They went outside to collect the bodies and stack them up.

THIRTY-TWO

The trail of the three horses led Clint and Wycliffe to Billy Dixon's ranch.

They reined their horses in.

"Damn it," Kelly said. "They rode right into the ranch."

"Looking for fresh horses, probably," Clint said.

"And trouble," Kelly said. "The boys ain't gunmen, Clint."

"We better go in quiet," Clint said. "I see tracks going in, but none coming out."

They rode over to a stand of trees and tied their horses off. Actually, Clint just dropped Eclipse's reins to the ground, knowing the Darley wouldn't move unless he really had to.

"What do you see?" Clint asked.

"We should be able to see somebody," Kelly said. "Ed was gonna look for mustangs to break. He should be at the corral."

"Maybe he's on the other side."

"Somebody would probably be in the barn."

"Okay, then," Clint said. "Let's hope we just can't see them."

They started for the house on foot.

Billy Dixon sat up and caught his breath at the pain the move caused. He was wrapped tightly, and stitched up, but he couldn't just lie there. Not with Clint and Kelly and who knew who else out looking for the men who shot him.

"Where do you think you're going?" the doc said, coming into the room.

"I've got to get out of here, Doc."

"And do what? You think you're gonna be able to sit a horse without tearing those wounds open?"

"I figure I'll try."

"You won't get a mile before you start to bleed to death."

"I've got to give it a try."

The doc stared at him, then said, "Okay, go ahead. Let me see if you can even make it to the door."

Dixon glared at the doctor, then lowered his feet to the floor.

"I'll need my boots," he said.

"If you can ride, you can put your own boots on," the doc said.

"Where are they, damn it?"

"Under the table."

Dixon looked and saw the boots under the examination table he'd been lying on.

"What the hell are they doin' there?" he demanded.

"Stop complaining. Just go and get them and put them on."

Dixon stared at the doctor, then bent over to try and get his boots. He reached for the boots, but couldn't stretch that far, and couldn't get down low enough to get under the table without tearing his stitches.

"Ahhhhhh, shit," he said, finally giving up.

"You want help getting back up onto the table?" the doc asked.

"Ain't you got a bed I can use instead?"

"I do," Doc said. "I keep it for patients who are going to cooperate. Is that you?"

Dixon leaned on the table and caught his breath.

"Yeah, yeah, I'll cooperate."

THIRTY-THREE

They circled around, figured to move in first from behind the house. Once they had their backs pressed against the back wall of the house, Clint risked a look inside the windows.

"Nobody, and nothing," he told Kelly.

"Bunkhouse next," Kelly said. "With me not here, somebody is for sure sleepin'."

"Okay."

They moved to the bunkhouse, pressed their backs to the wall. This time it was Kelly who peered in through the window.

"Looks like somebody was in one of the bunks," he said, "but not now. We move to that end of the bunkhouse and look out, we should be able to see around the corral."

Clint nodded.

Nobody was near the corral, in front or behind it.

"Damn it," Kelly said. "If they're here and alive, they might be playing poker on a hay bale in the barn."

"Let's hope they are."

"They are, I'm gonna hand 'em their asses," Kelly said. But Clint could tell he was worried about his friends.

They had a long way to go in the open between the bunkhouse and the barn.

"You go first," Clint said, "I'll cover you."

Kelly nodded. He broke from the cover of the bunkhouse and ran past the corral to the side of the barn. He waved at Clint to come ahead. When they were both alongside the barn, they tried looking between the boards.

"I don't see anything," Clint said.

"Me neither."

"Is there a back door?"

"Yeah."

"Okay, you take the back, I'll take the front."

"I got the badge, Clint."

"All right, then," Clint said. "I got the back. I'll move in when you do."

Kelly nodded, and they moved.

Clint got to the back door, cracked it, and waited. When he saw Kelly go in the front, he opened the door and stepped inside, gun held out in front of him.

"This is the sheriff," Kelly yelled. "Anybody in here?"

No answer.

"Boys, it's Kelly."

Still no answer.

They started looking in stalls.

"These two ain't our horses," Kelly said. "And they been rode some."

"So they did come here, and they got fresh mounts,"

Clint said. "The question is, what happened to your men?"

"I don't think I'm gonna like the answer."

They found them behind a stack of hay bales. All four of them, dead.

"Damn!" Kelly said, falling down to one knee.

"Looks like they got one of them before they died," Clint said.

Kelly angrily pulled the body of the bank robber away from the bodies of his three friends. Then he kicked it a few times.

"Goddamnit!"

Clint put his hand on Kelly's shoulder.

"I'm sorry about your friends."

Kelly looked at Clint with rage in his face.

"We're gonna catch these bastards!"

"Yes, we are," Clint said.

He knelt by the body of the dead bank robber, went through his pockets. His body had been stripped of anything that might identify it.

"He must have a saddle around here somewhere. Maybe some saddlebags."

They searched, found the robber's saddle, but no saddlebags.

"His partners must have taken it with them."

They walked outside. Clint studied the ground, walked a ways from the barn.

"Tracks clear up over here," Clint said. He came back to Kelly. "Why didn't they take some of the mustangs? That'd be a good animal to have in this terrain."

"Ain't been broke yet, none of 'em," Kelly said.

"We better stock up on whatever supplies you have in the house," Clint said. "Unless they thought of that, too."

"We got some stores hidden away," Kelly said. "In case of Indians, or Comancheros."

"Okay, then."

Kelly led the way.

THIRTY-FOUR

They decided not to take the time to bury the dead men. They'd do that on their way back, after they caught Garver and the other man. They covered them up as best they could and left them in the barn. They included the dead bank robber, so his body wouldn't attract any scavengers, who would then find the others.

"Look here," Clint said as they were covering him up separate from the others.

"What?" Kelly asked.

"He's shot in the hip, and the back."

"So?"

"So I'm wondering who shot him in the back."

"You think Garver took the chance to kill his own man?"

Clint shrugged and said, "Why wouldn't he? Makes for a bigger split."

"That'd be the way that kind of man thinks," Kelly agreed.

* * *

They mounted up, each carrying some of the supplies they'd found. They took water, coffee, beef jerky, some canned fruit, pans, cups, and a coffeepot. Kelly figured they should use one of the other horses as a pack animal, but Clint disagreed.

"That'd slow us down," he said. "I'm sure they're riding without a pack animal."

"I'd say you're right," Kelly said. "There's four of our animals missing, but if you look way out there, you'll see two of 'em, just standin'."

The foreman had good eyes. There were two horses standing off in the distance.

"They're waitin' for us to leave so they can come back," Kelly said.

"No point letting them stand out there, then," Clint said. "Can they make do with the water in the trough and the hay in the barn?"

"'Til we get back, yeah," Kelly said.

"Then we better start following these tracks."

"Clint?"

"Yeah?"

"You know what you said about bringin' them back alive?"

"I remember."

"I don't know as I can do that."

"Can't say I blame you for that, Kelly."

Garver and Wycliffe had ridden away from the ranch at a good pace.

"There'll be some kind of posse by now," Garver told Wycliffe. "Maybe even have the Gunsmith in it."

"When they reach that ranch and find those men, they'll really be after us," Wycliffe said. "Maybe we should split up."

"Now why would you suggest that?" Garver asked.

"Well," Wycliffe said, "maybe it's because I don't want a bullet in the back like Stanford got."

Garver looked over at Wycliffe.

"He was gonna die anyway," he said. "I saved him some pain."

"He was shot in the hip."

"Crippled, then," Garver said. "He would've slowed us down."

"Split the money and split up," Wycliffe said. "That's what I'm thinkin'."

"Let's get someplace safe," Garver said, "and then we can talk about it."

THIRTY-FIVE

Clint tracked Garver and the second man, hoping they wouldn't split up, but expecting them to.

Eclipse traveled easily beneath Clint, but he had suggested to Kelly that he get himself a fresh mount.

Kelly patted his horse's neck and said, "This is the best animal on the ranch. Besides, I'd have to break one of those mustangs, and it would just take too long. Unless you wanna break one?"

"Not me," Clint said. "I've never been a bronc buster."

"I'm not much of one either," Kelly said sadly. "That's what the other boys were for."

Now, as they followed the trail, Kelly said, "Can't we go any faster?"

"I'm a better tracker than I am a bronc buster, Kelly," Clint said, "but not by a lot. No, I can't go any faster."

"Well, they're headed east, right? Can't we just ride east?"

"The trail may change," Clint said. "They could change direction, or split up, and if we missed it, we'd lose them."

Kelly understood. He was still impatient, but he understood.

Half a day and thirty miles later Clint said, "There," and pointed to the ground.

"What?"

"They just changed direction," Clint said. "They're headed north."

"Indian Territory? Why would they go there?"

"Maybe they think nobody would be stupid enough to follow them?"

"Well . . . we are," Kelly said.

"Yeah, Kelly," Clint agreed, "we are. Maybe they'll switch and go west again, into Arkansas. We'll have to wait and see."

Kelly touched the badge on his chest.

"This tin won't be good in either place, will it?" he said.

"I wouldn't say no good," Clint said. "It still gives you some status. It gives us a legitimate reason to keep chasing them, no matter where they go."

"And that's what we're gonna do," Kelly said. "Wherever they go."

Clint had to force Kelly to stop for the night, to rest not only themselves, but their horses as well. They built a fire and Clint put on a pot of coffee and broke out the beef jerky and canned fruit.

"Take a deep breath," Clint said.

Kelly looked across the fire at him.

"What?"

"You haven't taken a breath since we left the ranch," Clint said.

"I can't breathe," the foreman said. "Not 'til we catch those bastards."

"If you don't breathe," Clint said, "you won't make it."

"If those were your friends, would you be breathin' easy?" Kelly asked.

"Not easy," Clint said, "but I'd be breathing, because that's what it's going to take. Have you ever tracked a man before?"

"No."

"Believe me," Clint said, "staying as tight as you are right now is not going to help us."

"Yeah, okay," Kelly said, "I get it. I understand what you're saying. I'll try."

"Let's take a watch each," Clint said, "just in case. You turn in first."

"I ain't tired."

"Trust me," Clint said. "By the time you put your head down, you'll be asleep."

As Kelly wrapped himself in his blanket and settled down, Clint put on another pot of coffee. By the time he was able to pour himself a cup, he could tell by the man's even breathing that Kelly was asleep.

He broke out another chunk of beef jerky and stared at the stars. He didn't expect there was any danger of anyone coming up on them, unless Garver and his partner turned around. There wasn't much chance of that. Not after they'd killed all those men at the ranch.

Clint knew how Kelly felt, but the man had to take it

easy or he was going to explode. He didn't want to have to go up against two killers with a man he couldn't rely on. Not like in the saloon, with Little Jim. Kelly had frozen.

He couldn't have that happen again.

THIRTY-SIX

"I'm thinkin' Arkansas," Wycliffe said.

"Why?" Garver asked.

"Because I don't wanna go into Indian Territory."

"What do you have against Indians?"

"You mean savages who scalp people?"

"Have you had any dealings with Indians?" Garver asked.

"Not much."

"Well, for the most part, they're not so bad. I mean, considering we've stolen their land and forced them onto reservations."

"Well, it ain't just the Indians."

"What else is there?"

"Judge Parker, and his deputies."

"We ain't done nothin' in the Territories," Garver said. "There ain't a reason for Judge Parker to be after us."

"The way I hear it, he ain't got to have a good reason to hang a body."

"So then why go into Arkansas?" Garver asked. "You'd be right in Parker's backyard."

"I'm just gonna ride through, and keep goin'," Wycliffe said.

"East? Ain't nothin' there."

"There is if you got enough money."

"Well," Garver said, "we got a lot."

"Yeah, about that," Wycliffe said. "Don't you think it's time we split? Or were you hopin' I'd catch a stray bullet and you wouldn't have to."

"Why do you have to be like that, Wycliffe?" Garver asked. "Sure, we can split the money up now."

Garver grabbed his saddlebags and pulled them over, prepared to stick his hand inside.

"Hold it."

Garver stopped. "You thinkin' I've got a gun in there?"

"You never know."

"I'm wearing a gun," Garver said. "If I was going to kill you, I'd just go for it."

"Maybe," Wycliffe said. He pressed his hands to Garver's saddlebags, but didn't feel the bulge of a gun in either one.

"Okay," he said, sitting back.

"I don't know what I did to make you so suspicious, Wycliffe," Garver said.

"Maybe it's the fact that you killed Stanford," Wycliffe said. "Or maybe I'm just naturally suspicious."

Garver took the money from the saddlebags and, by the light of the campfire, counted it and divided it.

"That's forty-four thousand, eight hundred—each," he said.

Wycliffe collected his part and stuffed it into his own saddlebags.

"We better stand watch," Garver said, stuffing his money back into his saddlebags. "I'll take the first and wake you in four hours."

"That's fine with me," Wycliffe said.

He took his saddlebags with him and cradled them while he lay down on his blanket and bedroll.

Both men slept that way, but neither of them got much rest that night.

Kelly woke Clint in the morning, with a fresh pot of coffee going.

"How are you doing?" Clint asked.

"I'm breathin'," Kelly said. "Thanks for the advice yesterday. I couldn't see past all the dead men."

Clint didn't think the foreman-turned-lawman was being entirely sincere.

"I don't expect you to forget the dead men, Kelly," he said. "Just tuck them away in the back of your mind until we finish this job."

"Oh, it's a job?"

"As long as you're wearing that badge, it's a job."

"Well then—" Kelly reached for the badge, and Clint stopped him before he could take it off.

"Leave it on!" he snapped. "You're a duly sworn lawman representing Adobe Walls. If you take it off now, who'll know? And you'd be leaving them without a sheriff."

Kelly stared at Clint, then asked, "Am I gonna get a chance to kill Garver?"

"Yes."

"Then okay," he said. "I'll do it your way."

"Good," Clint said. "I'll get the horses while you kill the fire and put away the pot."

THIRTY-SEVEN

Garver and Wycliffe rode together to the border between Texas and the Indian Territories.

"This is where we part company," Wycliffe said.

"Are you sure you want to do that?" Garver asked. He hated to see that other $44,800 leaving him behind.

"It's been fun, Garver," Wycliffe said, "but you're on your own now."

"Okay," Garver said, "if that's the way you want it."

"You go first," Wycliffe said.

"You really think I'd shoot you in the back?" Garver asked.

"I don't know," Wycliffe said, "why don't we ask Stanford?"

"I'm hurt, Wycliffe," Garver said. "I made you my partner, and I made you rich, and this is the thanks I get?"

"I'm real grateful, Garver," Wycliffe said. "but you go first."

"Okay," Garver said with a shrug. "See ya, Wycliffe."

Wycliffe watched his partner—his former partner—ride north toward the Indian Territories. He watched Garver until he was out of sight before he felt safe enough to ride east toward Arkansas.

Clint and Kelly got an early start. Clint figured by the tracks that they were about six hours behind Garver and his partner. He was pleased when they came upon the two men's camp five hours later.

"We're getting closer," he told Kelly.

"Five hours? That's closer?"

"It's closer than I thought we were," Clint told him. "That's what I care about."

"Then we should get goin'," Kelly said.

"Wait."

Clint walked around the camp, looking at the ground. He reached into the ashes of the cold fire and came out with something he showed Kelly.

"Bank bands from around the money," he said.

"Did they burn the money?" Kelly asked.

"No," Clint said, "they made their split here."

"And they stayed together?"

"Looks like it."

Clint mounted up. "Okay, let's get moving."

"Don't hold back because of my horse," Kelly told him. "We'll move at your pace."

Clint decided not to argue. Kelly would have to prove that he could keep up.

* * *

Several hours later, Clint reined Eclipse in and looked behind him. Kelly and his horse had fallen well behind, and he waited for them to catch up.

"Don't say it," Kelly said. "I know my horse can't keep up with yours, but come on. Your horse is a monster."

"Don't I know it," Clint said. "So what's the point of me moving at my pace if I have to wait for you to catch up?"

"You're right."

"So we'll move at your pace, and we'll still catch up to them. And we won't run your horse into the ground."

"Agreed."

"Good."

They started off again at a more reasonable pace for Kelly and his horse.

Clint halted their progress several hours later.

"What's wrong?"

"The Indian Territories are over that hill," Clint said. "Arkansas is that way."

"Where did they go?"

Clint stepped down from his horse and walked around.

"They split up here," Clint said. "One that way, one that way." He pointed to the Territories, and to Arkansas.

"So we split up?"

"Wait," Clint said. "I was never convinced that Garver was a true lawman. Given what he's done since then, I am convinced that he's a true outlaw."

"Meanin'?"

"Meanin' I want to travel each of these trails for a short time."

"And?"

"And that'll tell us something."

"What?"

"Let's find out."

They followed the trail that led to Arkansas for an hour and then Clint stopped.

"Well, we're not going to have to follow the trail to the Territories," he said.

"Why not?"

He pointed to the ground.

"I say it was Garver who headed for the Territories," Clint said. "He went north for a while, then he doubled back. Right here he came back."

"He joined up with the other man again?" Kelly asked.

"No," Clint said, "he's following the other man."

"Followin'?" Kelly looked confused. "Why?"

"Because, like I thought," Clint said, "he can't bear to see any of that money get away from him."

"So he's followin' his partner to rob him?"

"Bushwhack him," Clint said, "kill him, and take all the money."

"Sonofabitch."

"That must have been his plan all along."

"Wait," Kelly asked, "what about Little Jim? Why let him walk with his share?"

"I don't know, but I'll guess," Clint said. "I think he knew Jim was going back to town. He figured he'd be caught, his end of the take would be recovered, and maybe he hoped that the bank, and the town, would be happy with that."

"But they ain't," Kelly said, "and we ain't."

"That's right."

"So we're back on the trail of the two of them?" Kelly asked.

"Yes, but one of them is hunting the other one."

"Good," Kelly said. "I just hope they don't kill each other before we catch 'em. I want the pleasure of killin' one of them myself—especially Garver."

"We'll follow this trail," Clint said, "and take what we get."

Wycliffe knew he was being followed. What he didn't know was if it was a posse, or it was Garver. He wouldn't have put it past Garver to track him and try to take the money back from him.

But it could have been a posse. He had two choices. Run and try to put some distance between them, or stop, hide, and wait to see who it was.

He had to make up his mind.

THIRTY-EIGHT

Garver decided to take it slow.

He had drifted back in a southeasterly direction and picked up Wycliffe's trail, but he was in no hurry to catch up to his former partner. Better to lull him into a false sense of security, and then catch him off guard.

He would have preferred to end up with all the money, but allowing Little Jim to return to Adobe Walls was a calculated risk. Hopefully, the bank would be satisfied with 25 percent of their money back, and the law would be happy with Little Jim.

On the other hand, Little Jim might have killed whoever had initially replaced him as sheriff, and the town was still trying to find yet another replacement.

He stared down at Wycliffe's tracks. He was only about an hour ahead of him. He could close the gap anytime he wanted to. He had to decide whether he wanted Wycliffe to know he was taking the money from him, or simply ambush him so that he never knew what hit him.

* * *

"I don't understand what these tracks tell you," Kelly said.

They were each on one knee as Clint tried to give Kelly at least a rudimentary lesson in tracking.

"See the first track—"

"Okay, there," Kelly said, cutting him off. "How can you tell which one came first?"

"Because the tracker—I'm guessing Garver—is not being careful. See, his track overlaps the other. He's still following, and while both sets of tracks are hours old, I think Garver is still an hour or two behind his prey."

"Why doesn't he just bushwhack him and get it over with?"

"I think he wants to drag it out," Clint said, standing up. Kelly also stood. They both brushed dirt from their hands.

"Why?"

"He's probably trying to make up his mind."

"About what?"

"A man like Garver is bound to want his former partner to know it's him taking the money from him. He'd rather do that and see the look on his face than shoot him in the back and take it."

"Is this about his ego?"

"It's about pure ego," Clint said, "and, I think, pure evil."

THIRTY-NINE

Wycliffe saw the Indians up ahead of him, and reined his horse in.

Damn it, he had come this way to avoid the Territories in the north for just this reason. He didn't want to deal with Indians.

Since his knowledge of them was very sparse, he had no idea that he was looking at a band of Quapaw, who alternated between the North Territories and Arkansas.

He wasn't sure what to do. They were just watching him, and not making any moves toward him. He could keep moving forward, hoping they would ignore him, or he could turn around and go back the way he came. If he did that, he'd have to deal with either Garver or a posse—or both.

He could also head north or south, but one took him in the wrong direction and the other might take him toward even more Indians.

In the end he decided to keep moving forward, keeping his hands away from his weapons.

*   *   *

Garver could tell Wycliffe had reined in his horse for a while. What he didn't know was why. There was nothing about the horse's tracks to indicate it had injured itself. Perhaps he had seen something ahead, but had finally decided to continue on anyway.

Garver continued on as well. He had almost decided to follow Wycliffe until he camped, and take him then. Maybe even while he was asleep. To get the drop on him that way, and take back the bank money, would humiliate him greatly—and then he'd kill him. There'd be great satisfaction in that—and great profit.

"What's wrong?" Kelly asked.

"I don't know," Clint said. "They're stopping and going."

"Both of them?"

"Yes."

"Are they together again?"

"No."

"Then why?"

"I don't know," Clint said. "I guess it's all caused by the first man."

"Maybe he saw something that caused him to stop."

"Well, maybe we should keep going," Clint said. "The sooner we catch up to them, the sooner we'll find out."

A few miles later it was Clint who called a halt to their progress.

"What is it?"

"These tracks," Clint said. "Unshod ponies."

"Indians?"

"It would explain what the lead man saw that caused him to stop."

"But he kept going," Kelly said. "Would he do that if he saw Indians?"

"I guess that would depend on how many he saw," Clint said, "and what tribe they were."

"What tribe would be out here?"

"There are a few possibilities," Clint said. "Osage, Quapaw . . . a few more."

"Are they . . . dangerous?"

"Shouldn't be," Clint said. "They're most likely reservation races, unless . . ."

"Unless what?"

"Unless they're renegades."

Kelly looked around, as if he was suddenly worried that they were being watched.

"What if they're watching all of us?" he asked.

"Then maybe they're being entertained," Clint said. "Garver is chasing his former partner, we're chasing Garver. We probably all look like foolish white men to them."

"And do they kill foolish white men?" Kelly asked.

"I guess we'll have to find out."

FORTY

This time Clint actually saw the Indians—or at least, three of them—in the distance ahead.

Kelly saw them as well.

"How did they get there?" he asked. "Between us? Have they killed the other two?"

"Who knows?" Clint asked.

"Should we turn back?"

Clint looked at Kelly as they sat on their horses side by side.

"Would you be willing to assume that the Indians got your revenge for you and return to Adobe Walls?" Clint asked.

Without hesitation, Kelly shook his head.

"Okay, then."

"What should we do?" Kelly asked. "How do we find out who they are? What they want?"

"That's pretty simple," Clint replied. "We just ask them."

* * *

Clint rode directly toward the three braves. They stood their ground and waited.

"What are they doin'?" Kelly asked.

"They're waiting," Clint said. "They won't do a thing until we reach them."

Kelly touched his rifle.

"Don't touch your gun," Clint said. "Not unless I touch mine."

"There's only three of them," Kelly said. "We can take 'em."

"There's only three," Clint said, "that we can see."

When they got closer, Clint could see that they were young bucks, none of the three of them much over twenty. He didn't know if that would work for them, or against them.

"I'll do the talking," Clint said.

"That suits me," Kelly said.

"Oh yeah," Clint said. "Put that badge in your pocket."

"Why?"

"You don't want to tempt them with a target," Clint asked, "do you?"

Kelly took off the badge and put it in his shirt pocket.

"Hello," Clint said as they reached the three Indians. He thought he recognized their markings, but he asked, "Are you Quapaw?"

The middle brave nodded.

"We are pursuing two white men," Clint said. "They are criminals. Have you seen them?"

Again, the young brave nodded. The other two simply stared at them.

Then the center brave spoke.

"They do not travel together," he said. "They did not show us any respect, as you have. They did not speak to us."

"Have you killed them?" Kelly asked.

Clint gave him a sharp look.

"Why would we kill them?" the brave asked, looking confused.

"Never mind," Clint said. "Which way have they gone?"

"They go east," the brave said, pointing. "Why do they not travel together?"

"We believe one of them is hunting the other," Clint said.

"Why?"

"Because they are not honorable men," Clint answered. "They would kill each other for money."

"For money?" the brave asked. "Not for horses, or skins?"

"No," Clint said. "For money."

The brave honestly did not understand such actions. Or rather, such reasoning.

"What is your name?" Clint asked.

"I am Red Joe."

"Red Joe?" Kelly asked. "What kind of name is that?"

"Reservation name."

"It's a good name," Clint said.

"What is your name?" Red Joe asked.

"This is Kelly," Clint said. "I am Clint."

"Clint?"

"That's right."

"Kelly?" Red Joe said. "What kind of name is that?"

"Irish," Kelly said.

"Why do you seek these men?"

"I told you, they are criminals," Clint said. "They have also killed our friends."

"You seek revenge?" the brave asked.

"We seek justice," Clint said.

The braves turned to each other and conversed in their own language for a few minutes. Then the middle brave turned back to them.

"The men you seek are ahead of you," he said.

"We know," Clint said. "We are tracking them."

"We can take you."

"We can track them," Kelly said.

"We can take you short way."

"A shortcut?" Clint said.

"Yes," the brave said, "that is it. A shortcut."

"Why would you do that for us?" Kelly asked.

"Not do for Kelly," Red Joe said. "Do for Clint."

"Is that a fact?" Kelly asked.

"Never mind," Clint said. "I don't care who you're doing it for or why. "Thank you."

"This way," Red Joe said.

"What are their names?" Kelly asked, indicating the other braves.

"Not matter," Red Joe said.

"Why not?" Kelly asked.

"Not speak English," Red Joe said. "You not understand them, they not understand you. Not matter their names."

Kelly looked at Clint.

"Looks like you made a new friend."

The three braves started to ride off.

"We better follow them," Clint said. "While they're still in a good mood."

FORTY-ONE

Garver watched as Wycliffe made camp for the night. He had found a place where he could hide himself and look down at his former partner's camp. After dark he'd move in and get the rest of his money.

Wycliffe could feel the eyes on him, but didn't know if it was the Indians, or Garver. He put on a pot of coffee and made himself some beans.

And waited.

"It's dark out here," Kelly said.

"They know their way around," Clint said.

"Our horses could end up with broken legs."

"Not if we step where they step," Clint said.

Suddenly, the three braves stopped. Red Joe turned to look at them.

"You smell?" he asked.

Kelly sniffed the air.

"I don't smell nothin'."

But Clint did.

"Beans."

Red Joe nodded, then pointed.

"Over that hill."

"One of the men is over that hill?" Kelly asked.

Red Joe nodded.

"Which one?"

"The one that is not on the hill."

"So one man is over the hill making beans, and the other man is on the hill, watching him?" Clint asked.

"Yes."

"Then we're here."

"Yes."

"Thank you."

"You want we stay?" Red Joe asked.

"No," Clint said. "That's okay. We'll take it from here."

Red Joe nodded. He spoke to the other two braves. They actually smiled and waved, and then the three Quapaw rode off into the dark.

"What now?" Kelly asked.

"What do you want?" Clint asked. "The beans, or the hill?"

FORTY-TWO

They left their horses behind. Clint walked up the back of the hill. They didn't know where Garver was, top or bottom, but Clint assumed that Garver would not want to share the bank money with anyone. He figured Garver would be at the top of the hill.

He told Kelly, "You take the beans."

"I love beans," Kelly said.

"Better put your badge back on for this," Clint advised.

Kelly felt the weight of his badge as he advanced on the campfire on foot. He didn't know who he would find there, but he told himself he was ready.

Wycliffe heard someone coming toward his camp in the dark. He put his plate of beans down and removed his gun from his holster. He held it ready.

* * *

Garver looked down at the camp, saw Wycliffe sitting at the fire. He was about to head down the hill to the camp when he saw someone just outside the circle of light given off by the fire.

"Who the hell—" he said.

"That's a friend of mine," Clint said from behind him. "Actually, he's a lawman. He's got your old job, as a matter of fact."

Garver turned, saw Clint standing there.

"What the hell are you doing here?" he demanded. "What are you both doing here?"

"Oh, we came for you, and your partner, and the rest of the bank's money."

"You followed us all the way out here for that?" Garver asked.

"Well, not exactly," Clint said. "We also want you for shooting Billy Dixon, and killing his men."

"So you sneak up on me in the dark so you can bushwhack me?"

"Who said anything about bushwhacking you?" Clint asked. "I'm here to give you a fair fight."

"In the dark?" Garver asked.

"You saying you want to wait for the sun to come up?" Clint asked.

"That's exactly what I'm saying."

"So if I decide to agree, and wait 'til morning, you won't try to skulk away in the dark?"

"Skulking away in the dark isn't exactly my style," Garver said. "Besides, I think I can take you in a fair fight."

Clint thought a moment, then said, "Okay. I'll tell you what I'm going to do. I'm going to get my horse and take him down to that camp, where I'll wait for sunup. After that, you better come down from this hill, or I'll come up after you."

"Don't worry about me, Adams," Garver said. "I'll deal with you come daylight."

"I'll be ready," Clint said. Then he pointed his finger. "Don't make me come up here and get you, hear?"

"I hear."

Clint backed up until the darkness enveloped him, then he turned and walked down to his horse.

FORTY-THREE

Kelly stepped into the light, the badge plainly displayed on his chest.

"What the hell—" Wycliffe said. "Who are you?"

"Sheriff from Adobe Walls."

"Since when?"

"Since Garver shot down Billy Dixon in the street and robbed the bank with you and Little Jim."

"You been trackin' me all this time?"

"That's right."

"All these days? Because of the town's bank?"

"Billy Dixon is my friend, and my boss," Kelly said.

"The town sheriff has a boss?"

"I'm also the foreman of the Dixon ranch."

"Where the hell is that?"

"You should know," Kelly said. "You left four dead men there—one of your own."

"That place?" Wycliffe asked. "Look, I've got a lot of money in these saddlebags. I'll pay you—"

"No."

"You ain't heard how much—"

"No."

"Then what . . . you're gonna take me back?"

"Or kill you here."

"You can do that . . . alone?"

"I ain't alone," Kelly said. "I got the Gunsmith with me."

Wycliffe froze.

"Where is he?"

"Behind you."

Wycliffe's eyes flicked about in his head. He flexed his hand on his gun.

"You're lyin'."

"Try me," Sheriff Kelly said.

"I'll kill you," Wycliffe said. "You're no gunman."

"Go ahead, kill me," Kelly said. "You'll be dead one second after you pull the trigger."

Wycliffe thought the proposition over. Kelly could see the man's shoulders slump as he made up his mind.

"Dump the shells," Kelly said.

Wycliffe opened the cylinder, dumped all the bullets onto the ground.

"Now toss the gun into the fire."

"What?"

"Do it!"

Wycliffe frowned, then dropped his gun into the fire.

Kelly drew his gun and approached the man.

"Stand up, hands behind your back."

Wycliffe obeyed. Kelly stuck his gun in his belt, tied the

man's hands, then slid his gun out again. Wycliffe took the opportunity to turn around and look.

"Where's Adams?"

"He'll be along."

Wycliffe turned on Kelly.

"You bluffed me?"

Kelly grinned. "You said I'm no gunman," he told Wycliffe. "I guess that means you're no poker player."

Clint walked into camp minutes later, leading both their horses.

"Where's Garver?" Kelly asked.

"He'll be coming down at first light," Clint said, accepting a cup of coffee from Kelly. "Then we'll settle it."

"He's gonna come down willingly?" Kelly asked.

"Rather than have us chase him down eventually," Clint said. "Besides, the rest of the money's down here. He'll try to figure out a way to escape with all of it."

Wycliffe shook his head and laughed.

"What's so funny?" Clint asked.

"Garver's already miles away from here. You'll never catch him."

"You don't know him as well as you think you do," Clint said.

"I know him real well," Wycliffe said. "I knew he'd want all the money for himself. I knew he'd follow me and wait for a chance to take it."

"You were right that far," Clint said. "But trust me, he's not going anywhere."

"He's not gonna take on both of you," Wycliffe said.

He looked down at the pan on the fire. The beans had congealed.

"Kelly," Clint said, "you want to make a new batch of beans?"

"Sure, why not?" Kelly said. "A man's gotta eat, right?"

FORTY-FOUR

Wycliffe fell asleep, with his hands still tied behind him. His gun was still in the fire, the wooden grips burned away, the metal red-hot.

Clint and Kelly sat by the fire with coffee cups in their hands.

"You think he's really gonna come down?" Kelly asked.

"I think so, yeah," Clint said. "He knows we know what he did. If he runs, we'll chase him, and catch him."

Kelly pulled Wycliffe's saddlebags to him and looked inside.

"With a saddlebag like this, I might take the chance," he said. "Maybe he will, too."

"The chance he'll take," Clint said, "is that, somehow, he'll come out of this with all the money."

"And how's he gonna do that?" Kelly asked, setting the saddlebags aside.

"Beats me," Clint said. "I guess we're gonna find out."

* * *

Garver sighted down the barrel of his rifle at the camp. At the first sign of light he'd take his shot. He'd have them before they knew what hit them, and then the money would be his.

He waited.

At first light Clint and Kelly saddled the horses. They wanted to be ready to ride out as soon as possible.

"He should be down any minute," Clint said. "We'll get this done with and head back."

Clint looked up at the hill where he'd left Garver, saw the glint of the sun off something shiny.

"Down," he said to Kelly.

Garver started to squeeze the trigger, sighting on the Gunsmith first, but he stopped when he felt something hard press against the back of his head.

"Put rifle down," Red Joe said, "and stand up."

"Now wait—" Garver said.

"You stand up now," Red Joe said, "and we walk to camp."

Garver looked at the three Indian braves and knew his chance had passed. He looked down at the money.

"My saddlebags—" he said.

"He takes," Red Joe said, indicating one of the other braves. "We go . . . now."

"What the—" Kelly said.

Clint looked and saw the three Quapaw braves leading Garver down the hill. One was holding the saddlebags of money, the other his rifle.

"Guess there's been a change of plans," Clint said to Garver.

Garver looked down at the trussed-up Wycliffe.

"Sorry you didn't get the chance to plug me and take all the money, partner," Wycliffe said.

Garver didn't answer.

"Time to head back," Clint said.

"No," Garver said. "I want it to end here."

"If it ends here," Clint said, "it ends badly."

"If I go back, it ends at the end of a rope," Garver said.

Clint looked at Wycliffe.

"Don't look at me," he said. "I'll go back."

Clint looked at Kelly, who shrugged. Then he looked at Red Joe.

"All right," Clint said, "give him back his gun."

Watch for

BUFFALO SOLDIERS

362nd novel in the exciting GUNSMITH series
from Jove

Coming in February!

Bruce County Public Library
1243 Mackenzie Rd.
Port Elgin ON N0H 2C6